Do You Know Me?

short stories

by

Caro Soles

Baskerville Books

Table of Contents

Preface
7

Do You Know Me?
9

Beau Geste
15

The Messenger
23

The Chosen Few
31

Heart of the Garden
55

A Weekend in the Country
61

Bel Canto
83

Chops and the Stiff
113

The Secret Child
131

Chapter One – *The Danger Dance*
161

About the Author
175

Preface

This short book is an eclectic assortment of stories. Unlike most collections, here you will find stories written in many genres, some you may not be used to reading. From literary to science fiction to a little dark fantasy and even a touch of gay erotica, I hope you enjoy the journey as much as I did.

Some of these are brand-new stories, some have been published over the years in various anthologies. If the story is a reprint, I have explained where and when at the title page of each one to give a bit of context.

And here is where I get the chance to thank those supportive people who have helped with this book in some way. Thanks to Nancy Kilpatrick who gave me the encouragement to do this project in the first place. To Cheryl Freedman, whose keen-eyed copyedit rescued me many times over! To Istvan Kadar for his usual wonderful work on the cover. To all those editors who invited me into their anthologies, thus inspiring me to write these stories in the first place.

And last, but definitely not least, to all the readers who have sent me notes of support and especially reviews! I dedicate this to you!

Do You Know Me?

Do You Know Me?

"Hello."

The voice is metallic. Measured. Unaccented. I haven't heard it before and it scares me. I am used to the disembodied voices I hear from time to time in the darkness. But they are human. I think. This one? Unlikely.

"Hello."

Again.

Does he want a reply? It, maybe. Does it want a reply?

"Hello."

I take a deep breath and it hurts. It's better if I don't move. I listen. Nothing. I watch the spiders slowly circling in their odd dance on the curtains. They have long spindly black legs and tiny heads and they move awkwardly as if just getting used to their bodies. I don't mind them at all. By now, they are almost friends in my addled brain, or rather, an unusual form of entertainment.

From far away comes a more familiar voice, crying out, trying to connect. "Why are you doing this to me?" Pause. "Are you there?"

Am I here? I look up at the ceiling where shadows lurk. As I watch, a large circular thing moves slowly, slowly towards the dark window. I blink. It looks just like a spaceship. The spiders seem to be moving more animatedly. Maybe they see it, too. Maybe it's the mother ship?

"Hello…Hello." Gurgle. Gurgle.

That voice comes from behind me somewhere, perhaps

above me. How tall are these creatures? I glance at the spiders, but they seem unconcerned.

"Hello. Gur-Kel."

A name?

"Aar-Keh."

So, no longer anonymous. Somehow this is reassuring. I wonder if they're interested in my name, in who I am. What I am. That thought swirls away as I notice the UFO on the ceiling is being swallowed by a black shadow. It occurs to me that Gur-Kel and Aar-Keh may be from this place—the saucer that is fast disappearing. Will they be stuck here? Like me?

The two aliens are now conversing jerkily in their own language, a series of gurgles and clicks and beeps that sound vaguely familiar, as if I should recognize it, have heard it all before. But I can't concentrate. This is disconcerting. I seem to be shattering, pieces of me drifting off as I lie here. Where?

I hear a distant rumble that scatters them completely. I can't find any threads.

"Why are you doing this?" comes plaintively from far away as I drift off.

Suddenly alarmed, I open my eyes. A large shape leans over me. I feel hands on my arm, on my wrist. I stiffen. I hear a slur of words but I can't understand. Something rattles above my head.

I whimper.

"How's the pain?"

What? "I am the pain."

A rumbling noise comes from the shadows.

"Do you know me?" I ask.

The answer, if there is one, is swallowed up as someone cries out close by. Maybe they know. Maybe they can hear me.

"Do you know me?" I call, but even I know my voice is a mere whisper, almost not there, like the shadow of the pain.

"Do you know me?"

Beau Geste

Beau Geste

The Old Bag lived in a huge room with lots of window ledges and half-dead plants. There were always plenty of chairs and cushions crowding around and newspapers piled up everywhere. The Old Bag talked to herself a lot, and sometimes she talked to her husband, who now lived on the mantle in a hideous green vase. I never heard him talk back. Not once.

I used to watch her through the window from the fire escape and a couple of times through the crack in the door, which she left open a lot so she could keep track of Nosy Parker down the hall when he was making one of his frequent shuffle expeditions to the garbage cans out back. On special occasions, the alluring smell of cheddar cheese popcorn came wafting from her microwave, floating around corners, twisting up the stairs, unmistakably beckoning me down from the third floor where I was visiting the Fat Persian.

When I smelled that special perfume, I knew she was entertaining the Old Geezer who lived in the front room with his yappy dog, Fritz. She always closed the door and pulled the tattered old velvet drapes, too. Like I cared what catarumpus they got up to together.

It was that violent storm last fall that drove me inside. I was soaked to the skin and must have weighed another few pounds with all the wetness clinging to me. I could feel the onslaught of the water against my back, as if it was trying to strip me naked. She leaned out and scooped me up and made disgusting cooing noises. She wrapped me in a big towel she took out of her cedar chest. She lighted a small fire in the fireplace, although I don't know why she bothered. It was so small, an ant wouldn't have felt any warmth from it. But maybe it was just the idea of the fire that appealed to her. Women. Who knows with them? But I digress.

Anyway, when she opened a can of salmon, I soon forgot about the minute fire. It was Fancy Red Sockeye. My favorite. The kind you don't find much in dumpsters, you know. After that, I made it my business to drop in real regular and keep an eye on the Little Old Dear. She enjoyed the company. I never answered her back, either. Did I notice a few things not quite kosher around the place? A few things here and there my light-fingered pal may have picked up on the never-never for real? Like the salmon, perhaps? Who am I to judge.

So anyway, I was real upset when I leaped through the window on Wednesday and found the whole room full of big shoes and boots, cops and firemen and whatnot. First, I thought the Old Bag of Bones had keeled over on me, but no. There she was, sitting on her captains bed in one corner, her long skinny feet in the lace-up shoes barely touching the floor, sniveling her eyes out into a shredding tissue. She looked real bad, but not as bad as the Old Geezer, her beau, as she called him. He lay on the floor at her feet, his head at an odd angle, a blue-green bruise blossoming on his forehead.

"Do you always go out about 9:15?" asked the cop with the black furry head.

"Well, I always go down to Luigi's on the corner to pick up the *Globe and Mail*," she said. "We used to have it delivered when Oliver was alive, you know, but this way it gives me a reason to go out. And I usually have a few words with Angela in the coffee shop before coming back."

"And everyone knows about this routine?"

"Well, I don't expect *everyone* knows," she said, obviously taken aback by the thought that someone might be interested in her innocent morning constitutional.

There was a commotion by the door as a gurney was wheeled in, knocking over a pile of newspapers and a dried-out pot of mums. The Old Bag jumped and covered her mouth with both hands. Her eyes behind the tortoise-shell glasses were round like big wet buttons.

"Oh, poor Lester," she sobbed. "Poor dear man."

"Ah, could you move over there, ma'am?" Furry Head grasped her skinny elbow firmly and maneuvered her neatly past the corpse and over to the window. I noticed she was still with it enough to pull the chintz curtain across the alcove where she kept her hotplate and electric tea kettle.

I leapt up on the mantle to get a better view of the room, noting the usual film of grey dust was missing all around the base of the green vase. Odd. But my attention snapped back to Furry Head and the Bag of Bones as the policeman steered her back on track.

"Mrs. Saunders, if we could just—"

"I'm trying to give you some useful background," she said, bridling.

"Yes, I appreciate that. Now, could you tell me who else knew about your morning walk to get the paper?"

Nosy Parker, I thought, settling down on the mantel. Below my perch, the Old Geezer was being photographed and examined and I don't know what all by the troop of men and women who stepped about as if choreographed by Bob Fosse. But my attention focused again on the two by the window.

"Did Lester have a key, Ms...?"

"Mrs. Mrs. Saunders. Yes. It's no use expecting the superintendent to let you in if you lock yourself out by mistake. By the time she gets back from the bar, you'll be half dead of starvation."

"Not too reliable, I take it."

"I'll say." The Old Bag of Bones perked up for a moment, expatiating on the perpetual alcoholic haze of the hated super. "So that's' why Lester had a key," she finished up, dabbing at her eyes.

I crouched down, staring hard at the old doll. I happened to know there were other times when Lester used that key. Not only that, but the whole performance was a bit over the top. I began to have doubts about the Old Bag of Bones. The cop, however, seemed to be eating it up.

"He must have surprised a burglar," the cop said.

Sure. Had he looked around this dump? Like there was a lot to steal here, oh yeah.

"Poor dear Lester," she said. She was dabbing at her

eyes again. Her glasses slipped sideways. "He used to help me clean the silver every Thursday."

"Silver?"

I was wondering about that myself. I'd never seen any.

"Oh, just a small gallery tray of my mother's that I kept. A tea set and four place settings. Here." She opened the case on the small end table and gasped. What a surprise. They were gone. Had they ever been there?

Furry Head was writing it all down in his notebook.

The Old Bag stood with one hand covering her mouth. "The place settings were very old." Her voice quavered. "And there was a set of silver candlesticks, too," she added, glancing at the mantle. "I just noticed they're gone, too!" More quavering.

Oh, really. Such overacting. If I hadn't had my suspicions before, I was pretty sure now. I wondered what the Old Geezer had done to set her off. I looked back at the gurney where they were now examining the wound on the Geezer's nearly bald head.

"Blunt force trauma," one said quietly. "Hard rounded object, I'd say." He pulled the red blanket over the Geezer's face and they began to inch their way out of the crowded room.

On impulse, I lifted a long delicate paw and pushed the urn off the mantle. It fell with a satisfying clunk, right beside the cop with the notebook.

The Old Bag screamed and turned pale under her rouge. "You miserable creature!" she shouted, shaking her fist at me. "Get out! Go away!"

"Now, now," soothed the policeman. "Cats are like that, aren't they? Always pushing stuff off tables just for fun."

"Not him," she sniveled. "He did it on purpose. And after all that salmon I gave him, too! Traitor!"

Furry Head tilted his head and looked at her closely. "I think you better come with me, ma'am."

Oh, well. No time for regrets. I arched my back, stretched and leapt to the bookcase near the door. I looked back to see the two cops examining the vase, their gloves on. Once the Old Geezer was wheeled through, I swished my tail and followed.

I ran nimbly up the dusty stairs to the third floor. Time to visit the Fat Persian and her even fatter person. They dined well up there, assuming you like your tuna out of the can.

Beggars can't be choosers.

The Messenger

First published in *David's Place: an AIDS Journal*
San Diego, 1994

The Messenger

He wasn't an old man, barely passed his fortieth year, but he walked slowly. He looked ahead along the beach, his dark eyes drawing the details around him: the crag and rocks, the rhythmic roll of the waves falling over each other to break against the glistening pebbles far down the shore.

It was years since he had been back here, years since he had felt the tangy kiss of salt against his lips. Everything was the same, yet there were subtle differences he could just make out along the shore, details that didn't match the careful landscape of his memory. The old hotel had been pulled down, the post office moved. A row of cottages stood where he had played as a child in the long grass of the meadow below the lighthouse

A year ago, he had thought of himself as in the prime of life. Now his world had slid sideways, and there was nothing to hold onto anymore. After months of struggle and rage, followed by weeks of listless sorrow, he had arrived back here, almost shipwrecked by the uncontrollable swell of his emotions.

It was over. Here along the wild untamed coast of the Atlantic where he had come every summer with his parents, he had found peace. Or he thought he had, for a while. Now he felt restless, unsure, afraid. Perhaps he had given in, he thought, rather than accepted. His eyes followed the sweeping dip of a sea gull over the grey roll of the waves. He hoped the feeling of peace would return, leaving him free to finish his work.

The subject of this article was "The Messenger in Greek Drama": the one who brought the news, described the battles, all the stirring events too horrible to be shown on stage. All this the messenger re-created with his poetry, his memory so exact, whole speeches would be delivered verbatim.

The one who brought the news of his fate had no poetry. Perhaps medical men should read the classics. Perhaps Greek literature should be a required subject before doctors could graduate. He smiled, imagining the reaction to this proposal.

He paused to rest and sat down, carefully adjusting his narrow buttocks onto an accommodating curve in the convenient rock, planting his feet against the smooth slide of the stones. The tide was turning. Far out across the expanse of pebbles on the beach, past the hulking mounds of rock covered with the shifting coats of green-black seaweed, the mud flats stretched glistening in the cold sunshine, waiting to be submerged again. Even as he watched, he could see the water creep closer, each wave eating more of the land between them.

His gaze moved out to the horizon, then back along the shore to the irregular granite cliffs that jutted far out into the water, cutting off his view. A bright shape flitted across his line of vision, seeming to be half in, half out of the deep pool of water at the mouth of the big cave. He blinked to make sure his eyes weren't playing tricks on him. Over the weeks, he had learned to distrust his senses, to test them again and again, afraid to slip into that shadowed land where every sound could suddenly take on a nightmare shape. He squinted into the distance. The figure was stepping carefully across the smooth rocks, head down, arms balanced out to the sides. A boy, it looked like, his long fair hair lifting around his head in the breeze. If this was unreality, it might not be too bad. The man laughed suddenly, the sound so unusual these days that it startled him, as well as a gull perched on a piece of driftwood nearby. He turned as the bird rose shrieking into the clear sky. When he looked back, the boy, or whatever it was, melted into the shadows under the cliff. With a sigh, the man got to his feet and trudged up the beach, over the hills of pebbles flung up by centuries of tides, back to the small weathered cottage on the hill.

It was later that afternoon when he thought he saw the boy again. his fair hair on fire from the sun, the rest of him in the shadow of the wharf. The tide was in by now, and the boy seemed to be standing in a boat; at least, that was all he could think of to account for the odd way that the golden head appeared and disappeared in the deep cool shadows along the pier. On an impulse, the man stood up, pushing back the wooden chair that scraped along the floor. Resolutely, he swept his papers together, anchoring them under a smooth stone from the beach and started out the door. His sneakered feet slid in the long grass as he made his way down the hill and along the path to the pier. It was a hulking structure left over from the days when scows pulled in to load the stacks of logs hauled in from the woods by the truckload. But that was years ago now, and the wharf was half in ruins.

As his feet touched the white boards, he was almost running, his heart beating a little too fast. But when he looked around, there was no sign of anyone. Disappointment washed over him and was smothered at once. He had come out for a breath of air. He walked briskly to the end of the pier, where the boards were jagged, broken long ago by a hurricane that had tumbled and jammed the timbers sideways and upside down at odd angles. He watched a few old lobster boats, their wooden traps piled on the decks, bob quietly at rest in the harbor. Then he turned around and almost lost his footing. The boy stood right behind him.

"Hi. You want a ride?"

"A ride?" He felt stupid, staring at the young man as if he had never seen a blond youth before. The eyes were startling: dark around the edges, dark in the middle, and in between flecked with green and blue, like the ocean. He looked away.

"I thought you came down looking for me."

"No, I just— Yes, I did."

"Good." The boy smiled.

The man felt a small explosion inside, as if his heart were suddenly on fire. He tried to steady his breathing.

"My boat's right here. I'll go first if you like." The boy sped down the ladder, jumping to the deck of the old trawler with practiced ease.

The man came down much more slowly, taking his time. Now he could hear the engine throbbing softly.

"We'll go around the point," the boy said, casting off and revving up the motor. The deck shuddered under their feet.

"The currents are bad."

"I know the currents."

Odd, the man thought. He doesn't talk like a native. His voice was light, throaty, inviting; his gaze, direct. Now that they were on the water, there was no question what he wanted. If there ever had been.

"Warm in the sun," the boy said, taking off his shirt. "We'll anchor around the point and go swimming. It's nicer there. More private."

"Are you in the habit of giving total strangers a ride in your boat?"

The boy shook his head, the shaggy golden hair flying about, electric with energy.

"So I'm your first?" the man went on.

"Hardly that." The boy glanced at him sideways under his long lashes, the look testing, assessing, and something else beyond the man's experience. His bare arms were tanned, the muscles standing out hard as he spun the wheel, heading for the point.

After that, they said nothing, the boy intent on steering, the man content to watch the strong young back, the wide shoulders flowing down to slim hips, the stance casual, the weight on one leg.

"You're not from here," the man said finally, his curiosity getting the better of him.

"Neither are you."

Silenced, the man smiled and looked over towards the horizon where the water met the sky and the grey-blue haze. A few moments later, the boy cut the motor. In the sudden silence, the flash of the anchor was a bright sound. The boy turned and grinned down at him.

"The water is warm here," he said. "It's like a small pocket of the Caribbean." He unzipped his jeans and slid them down over his hips, kicking out of them as he turned and climbed on the narrow gunwale. His tanned feet looked long and delicate against the splintered wood. For a moment, he hung there, naked and beautiful against the horizon. Then he dove into the gently heaving sea, leaving the man alone.

For a while, the man watched the sun dance and beckon on the waves.

"No," he said turning his head away. "Not yet."

He waited for hours until the boat was almost stranded by the tide. Then, stiffly, he climbed out and waded to shore.

He was smiling.

The Chosen Few

From the anthology
The Future is Queer, Arsenal Pulp Press, 2006

*NOTE: This was written in the "Don't ask, don't tell" era,
before out gays were allowed to serve in the
U.S. military.*

The Chosen Few

The Merlin panel shimmered, sending out waves of dimpled color around the imprint of Liam's hand.

"This is bullshit." He started to pull his hand away, but Jamal's large black fingers pushed it back against the wall.

"Come on, man. You gotta go first. Don't be a chicken-shit."

The others immediately began to crow and cluck, flapping their arms, an animated khaki chorus.

"All right! All right! Bring it on!" Far from being upset by the ribbing, Liam saw it as a sign of acceptance.

The Cobras hadn't been together long. They were handpicked, an elite group, some gay, some straight, part of Attack Squadron 388. It was the first time openly gay soldiers had made it into a Marine wing group since the new policy had opened the doors four years earlier. Some, like Liam and his lover Jack, were back from serving in the Aladdin Offensive. Some had come from other units or were recruited from other bases. They had all been through a grueling six-week training period in the latest in weaponry and fold-wing aircraft at Fort Eisler, the Marine base in California, and tonight they were celebrating. Everyone had made it one step closer to the top secret mission that had been the gossip of the base for weeks.

"Merlin wasn't a fortuneteller, you know," Jack pointed out, balancing a sugar cube on top of the pyramid he was building.

"Yeah, yeah, who cares?" Jamal stuffed a wad of gum in his mouth and settled back in his chair.

Rachel poured more rum in her glass. "So ask already! Ask who's going to make the final cut."

"He can't ask about anyone but himself," Boomer said, tossing back a handful of peanuts. "That's the rules."

"There are rules?" Jack said. "Who knew?"

Liam pulled his hand away from the glowing panel to cuff his boyfriend playfully on the head, then placed his palm again on exactly the same spot.

"You are strong-willed and highly competitive, with much leadership potential," Merlin intoned suddenly.

"Yada, yada," muttered Jamal. "He's the great white hope of the rainbow nation."

"It's just getting stuff from his file based on his palm print, you know," Jack murmured.

"Dark clouds are gathering," Merlin's robotic voice continued. "Hold close those you love."

"Not in front of me," cried Boomer.

"Get over it, you arrogant het." Rachel punched him none too gently on the bicep.

"Danger surrounds you," Merlin's voice went on, impervious to the catcalls and cheers that greeted this latest announcement. "Curb your impulses. Things are not what they seem."

"Will I get picked to go to the top secret mission?" Liam asked, his voice deep and dramatic.

There was silence as they all waited for the answer.

"You are to fly with the eagles. Listen to their call only."

The colors on the Merlin panel flickered, then faded away, leaving nothing but the dull grey wall of the lounge. Liam withdrew his hand.

"Pile of crap," he said.

"I dunno." Jamal patted his new mustache with one finger. "He said you're goin', right?"

"Yeah," sneered Boomer." The politically correct choice."

"Nope." Rachel pushed her glass away and stood up. "He said 'fly with the eagles,' which I take to mean the Eagle Squad, not this mission. I gotta go. See ya."

"Hah, what does she know?" muttered Ramon, the youngest member of the group, watching Rachel make her way to the door with evident dislike.

Liam gazed steadily at Jack as though he were the only one at the table. "The Eagle Squad is gathering intel on the Ekvanistan Nations in the Balkans," he said.

"We should just drop a bomb on the fucking Ekies and get it over with," Squint said, his words not quite slurring yet. "They've been nothing but trouble for years, stirring up the entire eastern sector like they do, claiming to be religious and all."

"No way I'll be ordered to join the Eagles anytime soon," Liam went on, ignoring Squint. "I'll be picked for this mission. We both will."

Jack shook his head. "You have seniority and more combat experience than me."

"Bullshit!" Liam thumped the table with his fist. "You're a weapons expert with higher scores on the last Dar-Fisher tests than me."

"If you two are going to fight, I'm out of here," Jamal said.

"Me too," said Boomer. "It's embarrassing, right, Ramon?"

"We're not fighting," Liam and Jack said in unison.

Everyone laughed. Ramon, uncertain of the undercurrents, grinned nervously and ordered another round.

∞

Something big was in the air. Raw recruits had been pouring in for basic training, with more shipped to other Marine bases or airlifted out to God knows where. No one was talking. The Cobras had been special from the start, and now that the brass was looking for a chosen few for some new mission, it seemed obvious the chosen would come from their squad, or at least their wing group. Just how many would be needed, no one was sure. As the group grew more at ease with each other, they compared notes and the intel they had been able to gather, trying to piece together what the brass was looking for. Did it matter if you were married? Male? Female? Straight? Gay? Special sniper skills? Combat experience? Underwater training? Their group included all of the above. They knew they were being watched, graded according to some esoteric scale. But now the training was over. Surely that meant they would find out soon who had been picked, didn't it?

"We're going to be separated," Jack said gloomily to Liam as they met in the storeroom near M barracks later that night. It was hard to find any sort of privacy on the base and they had to be especially careful. Being out and proud was all very well on paper, but attitudes don't change overnight. The inclusion ruling was still new and they didn't want to be a test case.

"They're picking the best, Jack. That's us."

"You, yes. You're an experienced pilot, a first lieutenant, even have a medal or two. Me? I'm just—"

"Stop putting yourself down! You're a weapons specialist, first class, and you have combat experience, too. Have you forgotten how we met?"

Jack laughed. "Yeah. You came flying through a window in front of an exploding shell in that hell hole town with an unpronounceable name."

"Best jump I ever made!"

"First time you jumped my bones, that's for sure." Jack said.

Hearing footsteps outside the door, they lowered their voices.

"Why would the brass pick gays anyway?" Jack whispered.

"They want the place redecorated?"

"Could certainly use it."

"Stop worrying." Liam slipped an arm around Jack's shoulders. But he was worried, too.

This mission was important to them, a chance to prove themselves, a chance for real glory and recognition and a big boost to their careers. Liam had his eyes on a captain's bars.

∞

But next morning, his dream lay shattered like broken glass. He looked at the message on his PDA in disbelief. Negative! He hadn't made it, after all. Hubris, he thought. He had been so sure. Everyone had been so sure! What had gone wrong? The results were supposed to be secret, but no military rule could stop the gossip mill. Within an hour, Liam knew that Jack, Squint and Boomer had been picked, and Rachel, Ramon and Jamal would stay behind. As he moved numbly through the routine of his day, everyone assumed he was going and he neither confirmed nor denied their covert winks and nudges.

The more time that passed, the harder it was to admit the truth, even to himself. How could he tell Jack? He dreaded the evening when the Cobras would gather for their farewell drink. Would the others see him as the failure he saw himself? Some part of his brain knew how illogical he was being, but it made no difference. When he thought of Jack going without him, he felt a wrench of loss so strong, it was a physical pain in his gut. He couldn't lose Jack now.

The day dragged on. Bit by bit, information filtered through to him. He was wading through some hated paperwork when he received a message from Jack that the group was leaving at 1500 hours. Forty-five minutes! The brass was obviously trying to do this with no fuss. He thrust his files back in their folders, flung them into the desk and rushed off to find Jack. He had no idea what he was going to say, but at the very least, they had to work out the code they would use to communicate. In a harsh military environment where they were denied conjugal rights, where a big step forward was just to be accepted at all, text messages, instant photos, and a few stolen moments in the storeroom had got them through. So far.

Jack wasn't responding to messages. Liam checked Jack's bunk and their usual haunts. No one had seen him. Time was running out. He headed for the storeroom near M barracks.

As he opened the door, the smell hit him. Deep retching noises echoed off the metal walls. "Jack? Jack!" He rushed forward, alarm flooding his brain. But it wasn't Jack he found, but Boomer, crouched on all fours on the metal floor. The big Cajun pulled himself away from Liam's outstretched arms and threw up again onto a crate of gun casings.

"Shit! We'd better get you an ambulance," Liam said.

"No! Don't tell them…" Boomer stopped, gasping for breath, his face gray and slick with sweat. He was so weak, he could barely hold his head up. Drool dribbled from one corner of his mouth. He seemed shrunken inside his uniform. Around his neck was the electronic ID card identifying him as one of those chosen for the mission, its holographic insignia glinting in the dim light.

They'll need a replacement, Liam thought. He glanced at his watch. It wouldn't be possible now to contact the number of people necessary to change Boomer's name for his on the crew list, would it? Boomer. He didn't even know the man's real name. Twice he had caught him knocking back painkillers by the handful, but Jack had talked him out of reporting the guy, even though he was one of the few in the unit who let the odd homophobic remark slip out. Boomer had been injured at Jumbalya four months earlier and the pain still ruled him. Had he taken too many pills? Mixed some deadly cocktail to chase away the pain demons before embarking on the mission?

Liam pulled out his PDA and accessed the medic alert number. Something made him pause.

"Don't tell…" Boomer tried to reach out to stop him but didn't have the strength.

Don't ask, don't tell. The outdated phrase echoed in Liam's mind. "You're burning up," he said, touching Boomer's forehead. "What did you take?"

"Just a little somethin' to take the edge off." Boomer opened his hand and an unmarked pill bottle spilled out.

"You fucking asshole," muttered Liam, furious that this druggie had been chosen instead of him. "What the hell was in there?"

"What do you care? Whadda…fuck…" Boomer's eyes flickered, then rolled up in his head. The big man slipped sideways, slowly crumbling to the floor.

Liam stood looking down at him, his brain racing with possibilities. At last, he reached down and felt for a pulse. There was one, but it was faint.

"Fuck!" He slid the ID key from around Boomer's neck, pocketed the man's PDA and left, closing the door softly behind him.

Back at his own bunk, he hurriedly packed his duffel, throwing things in helter-skelter, not giving himself time to think. If things were going according to schedule, he could just make it to the assembly point spelled out in Boomer's PDA. Everyone expected him to be there. With any luck, no one would do more than a headcount. But when he got to the heliport, jeep tires spinning on the wet ground as the rain closed in, the main 'copter had already left. Three other servicemen arrived at the same time, running over to huddle with him under the shelter of Hanger Two. He'd seen them around the base but didn't know them.

"If it ain't the homo hero," the tall one muttered under his breath.

"You with CSU, sir?" the redhead asked, wiping rain off his face.

Liam nodded.

"What'll we do? Call the brass?"

"Not necessary." Liam outranked them, thank God, since the last thing he wanted was someone checking the passenger list. Ramon, he thought suddenly. The boy would do anything for him. But jeopardize his career? Only one way to find out. He punched in an urgent message to Ramon on his PDA.

∞

Five minutes later, Ramon appeared, clutching two chopper key cards. "Come on, sir." He motioned them to the next hanger. "I can fly a Hawk 9 through any storm. No sweat."

Bless the corps for training marines to obey without question, Liam thought, following the young man. This was something that had always given him problems. The chopper looked threatening, looming above them on the damp asphalt.

"Are you sure you can make it out to the ship and back in this thing? It's pretty far out and the weather's getting worse."

"Just tell me where."

"USS *Phoenix*. Aircraft carrier."

"Never heard of it. Coordinates?"

Liam read them off.

"Piece of cake." Ramon jumped into the helicopter. His hands blurred over the instrument panel as he went through the takeoff routine. Liam heaved his duffel inside and climbed up after the others, his nerves singing with tension.

"Can't you go any faster?" he snapped.

Ramon's dark eyes looked back at him reproachfully, but all he said was, "Buckle up."

The ride seemed to take forever. Liam has been right about the weather. The wind picked up fiercely and rain gushed out of the sky. The sea, barely visible beneath them, heaved into high peaks like mountains. The other three seemed unconcerned. They ignored him, joking amongst themselves as the rain pounded against metal all around them. Liam kept seeing Boomer's body slumped over on the cement floor, drool hanging out of one corner of his mouth. And him, doing nothing to help. Thinking only of himself, and Jack. Or was it raw ambition that let the man die at his feet? If he was dead…

∞

By the time they landed on the *Phoenix*, he was so stiff with tension, he could barely climb down the ladder. The wind was howling even louder now, and he had to shout to make himself heard. For one wild moment, the way back to the safety of the base beckoned as he gazed at Ramon's anxious face hanging out of the cockpit. But he hadn't gotten this far by taking the safe road. He returned Ramon's salute and hurried through the torrents of rain into the ship with the others. The vessel shuddered and pitched in the weather, lurching against the sickening swell.

The mission ship was a surprise. Its size was impressive, but it felt neglected. No one greeted them, no security questioned who they were. Grey paint was peeling from the walls in the narrow corridors. The brick-red floor was faded from many years of wear.

"Not exactly shipshape, is she?" muttered the redhead.

Just as they had given up on a welcoming committee, a young seaman appeared and greeted them with a sketchy salute.

"You're late, sir," he said to Liam, his voice high and strained in the wind. "Follow me. I'll take you to your quarters."

He guided them down another corridor, through a door and into a long dormitory of bunks three deep. Liam's companions stayed there, while he was ushered to the end of the room to one of the tiny cells reserved for the junior officers. While he stowed his duffel in the footlocker, the sailor started to copy Boomer's name, rank and serial number onto the card on the door.

"Wait. The ID cards must've gotten mixed up," Liam said, showing his dog tags. The seaman made out a new card without question, slipped it onto the door and left.

Liam fell a new rush of energy as he watched the young man disappear. Protocol meant reporting for duty to the captain, but he had to see Jack first. If they were going to discipline him, he needed the picture of his lover's smile of welcome to take with him to the brig.

Jack wasn't answering his texts, so Liam checked the other cards along the corridor. Jack's name wasn't among them.

"Looking for your boyfriend?" one of his traveling companions asked as he squeezed by.

Liam stopped and gave him a long look. "Looking for your boyfriend, *sir*," he said.

The smile disappeared from the kid's face. "Sorry, sir," he mumbled.

As Liam continued his search, he noticed the usual surveillance cameras everywhere, but no one hailed him or questioned who he was or where he was going. Was no one monitoring the ship now that they were out to sea, heading for their strike target? Where was the crew?

As he emerged onto Deck C, a voice finally challenged him over the ship's speaker system. But it wasn't the captain he was ordered to report to. It was the first officer. Strange, he thought. A young ensign arrived at that moment, and he followed her to the officer's ready room. She opened the door, announced him and withdrew.

"You fucking idiot!" thundered the man behind the desk.

"*Davy?*" Liam stared at the red-faced man who had once long ago been his lover.

"Don't you Davy me, you stupid bastard!"

"Well, don't fall all over me with kisses, Commander," Liam said, but a cold shiver started down his spine.

"Moron!" Davy slumped back in his big leather chair and covered his face with one big hand. "Sit down."

Liam sank into the only other chair in the cabin. Davy looked older, much older than when they had first met. Liam had been nineteen when he encountered Davy Lindstrom in a bar in Atlanta. The place was off the beaten track, and Liam was working part-time to supplement his college money. It was lust at first sight for both, but the older man was already a naval officer with a lot to lose and feared for his career if their affair became known.

But that had been ten years ago at least. Why all this anger? It seemed far too extreme for what he'd done surely? Or at least for what Davy thought he had done. For an instant, Boomer's sweat-soaked face flashed into his mind's eye and he winced.

"You always were an impulsive S.O.B."

"I thought that was one of my more endearing characteristics."

"Asswipe." Davy shifted his weight and gazed at the row of monitors lining the wall to Liam's right. Storage holds filled with weaponry and stretches of narrow empty corridors flickered on the screens.

Liam studied the full face he had once known so well, the generous mouth, the unruly iron-grey hair that refused to lie flat. The normally bright blue eyes were dull with exhaustion, and there was a drained, pinched look around Davy's nose that had never been there before.

Liam leaned forward, his elbows on his knees. "What's going on here, Davy?"

The older man shifted again and sighed. "You've really stepped in it this time," he said at last." I don't know what stupid stunt you pulled to get here, and I don't want to know."

"If I wasn't here, you'd be a man short," Liam said.

"I wish we were."

"Look, it's obvious you don't want me here for some personal reasons I can't begin to fathom. I should be talking to the captain anyway." Liam got to his feet.

"The captain blew his brains out four hours ago. I'm in charge."

Liam sat down again. Something about Davy's haggard face made him hesitate to ask any questions. "Why wasn't I chosen for this mission?" he asked at last.

"Because you were down for something else is what I was told."

"The Eagle Squad?"

Davy nodded.

"But they're not slated back for months yet. How long will this mission last, anyway?"

"Look around, you idiot. This is a death ship. No one is coming back."

Liam took a deep breath. He looked at the monitors, at the big old-fashioned ship that had obviously been pulled out of mothballs for one final run. He thought of the captain who killed himself because he couldn't bear sending his unsuspecting crew into certain death.

"This is a joint operation, right? So how did they pick the crew?" His voice was a rusty whisper.

Davy sighed. "Nearly every one of us has special skills. Some, like me, volunteered with eyes wide open, rather than face a long slow death from an incurable disease. A few are here instead of being court-martialed."

"And Boomer Kinkowsky? Why was he picked?"

"According to his record, the man is fearless. I gather he's apparently addicted to painkillers, but honestly, what does that matter here? It's a way for him to go out with honor. There are others in the group you could say the same thing about. Too much booze, pills, dope. Whatever. They hide it well, but eventually, the weakness would win."

"God, what fools we were trying to excel. All along, they were looking for weaknesses."

"You've landed in hell, boy. And there's nothing you can do about it."

"All we wanted was a chance to serve, to show what we could do."

"You've got that in spades," Davy said.

"That's why there are so many gays in this unit? Because they knew we'd welcome the chance to fight?"

"Who knows? You see any gold stars of the Admiralty on my shoulder boards?"

"You do know the target, I take it?"

Davy snorted. "Always the cheeky one." He settled back and folded his hands across his stomach. "We're attacking the Al Forleze on Stasia Island. Headquarters of the Tronem Cult, which is secretly backed by the Ekvanistan Nations and used as a refuge for their terrorist leaders. Or so we were told."

"The Ekies! The bastards who dropped bombs on our hospital bases in—"

"Right. This is the first move in Operation Hannibal."

"So who are we? The elephants?"

Davy shrugged. "More like mallards. We're the decoys. We take their minds off everything else back on the mainland while our Second Army moves into Ekvanistan through the mountains in a pincer movement to take the other three leaders of the Ekies. They've been getting in place for this for weeks."

"So that's where everyone was going."

"It'll bring the Ekies to their knees at last."

"And no way they'll notice this dinosaur creeping up on them."

"Which is why we have ten supersonic Demon Deltas hidden on Deck B."

"So that's why we spent so much time training on the things. I should've guessed." And that was where Jack came in. Weapons expert, trained almost exclusively on the stealth Demons.

"Can you drive the damn things?" Davy asked.

"Yes."

"The idea is to bomb the hell out of them at low altitude, so you can't miss. Then, after the first run, you fly a loaded plane into the mountain."

Davy shoved a pile of surveillance photos across the desk towards Liam, showing a mountain stronghold built into the side of the cliff.

There was silence as Liam looked them over. "So this really *is* a one-way ticket," he said.

"I told you, boy. You backed the wrong horse this time."

Silence stretched out between them for a few moments. The old ship strained and creaked through the storm, eating up the knots, going full throttle with no need to conserve fuel or engines.

Davy rolled his shoulders. He pulled a mickey out of his pocket and offered it to Liam, who shook his head. "We don't have a lot of hours left." He glanced at the wall of instruments and monitors. "The old tub is making pretty good time."

"The last briefing we had, the Ekie leaders were still in Algiers," Liam said. "That was two days ago. They've gone back?"

The commander shrugged. "Probably misinformation. Our orders came in three days ago, straight from the top."

"Nothing since?"

"Nothing. At 1300 hours they were still giving us the green light in spite of this damn storm."

Liam stared across the desk as the ship pitched and yawed. So that was the dark shadow in the man's eyes: not the sickness that was slowly eating away at him, but the knowledge that his people were being sacrificed.

"Look, Davy, why do this? Why not hijack the planes and take off?"

"You're crazier than I thought." Davy started to laugh, then sputtered into a coughing fit. "And go where? Any idea how those things eat up fuel? Shit, isn't this why you enlisted? Why you volunteered for the elite Cobra unit? Why you did whatever you did to get on this damn tub when you weren't even chosen?"

Liam shook his head.

"Our orders on board are to wait, but you and I both know it's doubtful that any of the Demons will get back. Even if you do, this old tub will be blasted out of the water by Ekie missiles as soon as they realize what's happening. We're not going home again, either."

"And who knows about this?"

"As far as our guys are concerned, senior bridge crew only. I don't know when you guys will be briefed. Soon, I imagine. Orders direct to PDA."

"Shit. Bastards don't even have the guts to do it face-to-face." Liam watched the monitors, the images filling him with despair. Until one image flickered past. "Stop! Reverse! Get that image back!"

Davy flipped the switch and the landing deck came into focus. The Hawk 'copter from home base hung twisted and misshapen in the flashes of lightening, a twisted wreck, with Ramon's crushed body hanging from the cockpit.

"What the hell…"

"Sorry, Liam. We've only got a skeleton crew and can't spare anyone to take away the body. It's tricky landing in heavy weather. Almost impossible to take off again. A sudden updraft must've slammed him against the ship's tower, snapping off the propeller."

Liam jumped up. "I've left a trail of bodies to get here," he said, "and I didn't do it all to commit suicide. Where is Jack now?"

Davy brought up the ship schedule on his monitor. "Deck B, checking gear. Look, I'm sorry you're here, but now you are, there's nothing to be done. Go find your lover. You can die together in battle, which is, after all, what so many of us have fought for.

"But not as throwaways in a fake battle while the big boys do something more important!"

"You'll take out some of those terrorist types on Stasia, if that makes you feel any better."

"Yeah, sure. I'd feel better if I knew for a fact that Mr. Big and his cohorts were going to be there." Liam continued to stare at the image of the 'copter.

"It's no use," Davy said, his voice tired.

Liam stood abruptly and headed for the door. "Give me the schemata of the ship. And a list of our wing crew."

"Knock yourself out." Davy threw him a small data sheet. "You now have less than one hour before scramble."

They could've sent several automatic drones loaded with bombs, Liam thought angrily as he made his way through the silent ship to Deck B. Why sacrifice people?

The answer came to him almost at once. A drone couldn't handle the fancy flying this mission would demand, not at the speeds needed for surprise. Certainly not in this weather. And the Stasia forces wouldn't expect a suicide attack from a big ship like this, even if they noticed the Demons on their satellite feeds with the heavy cloud cover. Flying under the radar would catch them by surprise. The fool scheme might actually work.

∞

Jack was taking a break with his group when Liam found him. He jumped up and ran over to Liam. "You made it after all! I knew you'd get here somehow!"

"I made it." Liam put an arm around Jack and drew him away from the others. "Look, what I'm going to tell you has to remain between us, understand?"

"What's the matter?"

"Swear!"

"Sure, love. I swear. What is it? You proposing again?" He laughed.

"Shut up and listen." As Liam told him what he had learned, he watched the color drain from his lover's face.

"You trust Davy?"

"I do. We've got to get out of here. Now! Come on. The 'copter's wrecked, but we can take one of the Demons and get to an island."

"With a load of bombs."

"Dump 'em over the ocean. The fuel will last longer that way."

"And they have landing strips on this friendly island?"

"Stop grinning like that! I'll risk it."

"The U.S. Navy will come looking for us," Jack pointed out. "Face it, hon. No one will shelter two gay deserters. And that's what we'd be."

"Jack, we've got to try. Come on!" He tugged his lover out the door and started down the corridor. "At least, we'll be alive."

Jack pulled away. "No."

"They've made fools of us, don't you understand?"

"No, love. I'm where I want to be. Where I've dreamed of being since I was a kid."

"Jack, we don't have time for this." As if to back him up, the battle stations alert played out loud and clear from the ship's loudspeakers.

"I can't leave my crew," Jack said.

"Oh, for God's sake, it's a fucking suicide mission we weren't even told about. There's no oath of loyalty that covers that."

"I will not be the first gay officer to desert his post."

"Don't I mean more to you then some abstract principle?"

"I volunteered."

"For service in the special unit, yes. Not a secret suicide mission. Look who they've chosen, Jackie. Doesn't it strike you as odd that out of a group of twenty-eight, there are thirteen gays? Isn't that just a tad suspicious?"

"They picked the best people for the job. Like usual."

"Look, we're not the brave, the proud, the few. We're the halt, the lame, the gay."

"It doesn't matter!"

"It does! It's like ethnic cleansing! They're using us and throwing us away. Is this the new army you always dreamed about?"

"It's the one I'm in," Jack said stubbornly.

"Christ almighty! I'm trying to save you, you fucking idiot!"

"Liam dearest, I'm a marine. This is what I've wanted all my life. Only recently has it been possible. And now you're trying to take it away from me?"

"I want us to be together."

"We are. We're the chosen."

"I wasn't! I followed you."

"You *what*?"

"I took Boomer's place so I could be with you."

"Well, here you are," Jack said, shaking his head, a sad smile on his face. "You impetuous fool, you." He took out his PDA and checked the orders that flashed across the screen, then slipped it back inside his tunic. "I love you." He leaned close and kissed him tenderly. "*Semper fi.*" Then he turned away and started towards the door.

"Jack!" Liam's shout echoed eerily along the deserted corridor.

His lover paused, half turned and looked back, his athletic body outlined against the driving rain hitting the deck outside. He held out his hand.

Liam walked towards him and took hold of his hand and held on tight as they walked together onto the deck where the first of the Demons rose from the deck below into the swirling grey storm like some futuristic ghost.

Heart of the Garden

From the anthology *365 Scary Stories,*
Barnes and Noble, 2001

Heart of the Garden

It isn't a baby. We just call it that 'cause it sounds so safe. Normal. Suburban, you know? Sure. Like everyone has a small grave in the garden that oozes salt tears and moans in the night, right?

You know, when we bought the place, we got it cheap. An estate sale or something. Anyway, we didn't mind Baby's grave at first. He didn't want much. Just a little attention. The sound of my voice would calm him right down. The touch of my hand against the earth and the tears would stop. Of course, in the winter it might get rough, but hey.

Then one night, me being there just wasn't enough. The moans and cries got really loud. I was kneeling, my finger against my lips, patting the earth. I mean, I was worried about the neighbors, you know? They might think Sam was beating on me or something. Anyway, there I was in my housecoat with my face practically on the ground when I saw the earth move. Well, I tell you I jumped back so fast, everything was a blur. Really gave me a start! But the crying kept on, so I had to do something. A soother, I thought. Babies like soothers. I grabbed the dog's ball. the rubber kind with a squeaker inside. I pushed it into the soft earth. It came hurtling back at me…hard. It woulda been funny if it hadn't been so weird. I musta laughed sorta crazy and loud 'cause a light went on next door. Jesus Murphy! Next I tried the dog's bone. There was still some meat on it and maybe that's what made it appealing. Whatever, the bone stayed down. I went back to bed.

A week later, I was out getting the flower beds ready for the annuals. I was surprised to hear the sobbing begin. He usually held off till it was dark. Maybe the changing of the seasons was confusing him. This time, I went right inside and got a bone from the rib roast we'd had on Sunday. It was Sam's birthday, you know. That man sure loves his roast beef. So I thrust the bone straight down into the earth. Then I stood back and watched that thing sucked into the soil like some great animal was pulling on it.

"Ya know, hon, maybe we should check out what's really down there," Sam suggested, when I told about Baby's new trick.

I shook my head. "The real estate guy said it was somebody's pet cat. Like years and years ago. There wouldn't be anything left now."

Sam shook his head. "Must be something, hon."

I had to agree. Besides, Baby was gettin' kinda expensive tastes. On the other hand, it *was* a grave....

It went on like that for a while longer. I'd take out some scraps from dinner and for a while that keep the crying away. Then one day the scraps weren't enough. It was about nine o'clock and dusk was dropping around us and the crying was soft and pitiful like someone just lost their best friend in all the world. The neighbor's cat had killed a robin and I was holding the still-warm body in my hands as I knelt beside Baby. The cat crouched nearby, watching.

"Scram," I hissed, as I laid the tiny body on the ground. I was going to go back to the house to get some macaroni and cheese for Baby when the earth caved in and the bird disappeared. I just stared. Next thing I know, the cat leaps after it and then… No more cat. It was obscene the way the ground heaved up and down for a few seconds, then was still.

"Hon, maybe it's time," Sam said, watching.

I put my hand on the ground and felt a tremor, almost like a heartbeat. "Be gentle, Sam."

He came back with a shovel. We didn't have far to go before we saw Baby. Well, I guess we'll have to find another name for him. Baby doesn't suit a garden gnome. Even if he is buried. Even if he doesn't look much like one anymore.

Still, what do you think of the name Attila?

A Weekend in the Country

From the erotic anthology *Don Juan and Men*,
MLR Press, 2009

A Weekend in the Country

I can't remember a time when I didn't love him, hate him, sometimes want to thrust a stiletto into his black heart. He has ruined my life but I do not want to live in a world without my lord, Count Andrei Alexandrovitch Rubikov.

Even here in America, so far away from our Mother Russia, he is a magnet for all in society. He fits in here; I do not. They court him, flatter him outrageously for his looks, his wealth, his title. Me, they look at sideways, trying not to see what I am, what I long for, lest it contaminate them, make them see my lord in a darker light. I watch them trying to place me: not a servant, yet not quite an equal. There is no title before my name, yet I am at ease in society, know everyone he knows. And I know his secrets. Sometimes I think this shows in my eyes and it scares them.

As I stand near the half-open door to the Streussers' ballroom, I watch him through the potted palms, the curly ferns reaching out to tickle my cheeks. I see Andrei swing his blushing partner expertly into the next waltz, watch his full lips moving as he tells her lies, watch his green eyes slide away to fasten on the figure of her lanky, dark-eyed fiancé, Paul, standing in a group of young men, laughing. I see their eyes meet and watch the young man's laughter fade away as his gaze is held captive by the hunter. I know that look. Even though it is not directed at me now, I can feel the force of it, as if my body is attached to Andrei in some way, as if an unseen web is vibrating between us. My heart lurches.

The music rolls on, spilling out the door of the ballroom into the garden of the huge country house on the Hudson where Andrei and I are guests for the weekend. And then the dance is over and he's brought her back to her seat on the other side of the palms. She is not an attractive girl, hardly even a girl anymore, but her heavy face is flushed and her eyes sparkle. Bathed in the reflection of Andrei's charm, she is almost pretty.

"Thank you, *mademoiselle*," he says, bowing over her hand. The diamond pin of the order of St. Dimitri flashes on his chest. "You are a lucky man, *monsieur*," he goes on, turning to the fiancé, Paul.

He blushes, though whether at the compliment or at the heat of those green eyes, it is impossible to say. "I know that, sir. Sometimes I pinch myself to see if it's all a dream."

"A lovely dream to be enjoyed while it lasts," Andrei says.

"While it lasts?" Paul's shoulders straighten, his chin rises. He is not as tall as Andrei. He looks like an adolescent beside him.

"Of course, my dear sir. It will be over once you are married, no? She will not be your fiancée then, but your dear wife?"

The young man relaxes and laughs and glances at his young lady, who fusses with her dance card, crossing off a name, adding another as she chats with the young man who has come to claim his dance. The music changes to a foxtrot, a dance made popular recently by the Castles.

"Do you enjoy a good cigar, by any chance?" Andrei asks Paul. "I am becoming quite the aficionado with the help of your soon-to-be father-in-law." He moves between Paul and the other young men, effectively cutting him away from his friends. Like a sheepdog rounding up strays.

They stroll out into the garden and he sees me.

"Misha! Join us for a cigar." His eyes are bright with the light I recognize all too well. My presence will give Paul a false sense of security. My frustration will fuel Andrei's desire for the other.

"When the wolf shows his teeth, he isn't laughing," I say in Russian.

He smiles wider, his sensual lips glistening in the wavering light of the one gas lamp at the side of the red brick path. "Misha and his Russian proverbs," he says, moving closer to Paul to show his allegiances is with him, the new friend, not with me.

"What does it mean?" Paul accepts the cigar from Andrei, reaches for the cutter on his watchchain.

"It means that he is sulking," Andrei says. "It means he worries too much, *mon cher*."

Paul does not seem to notice the endearment as he clips the end off his cigar and moves along the path beside Andrei.

"It is difficult bearing the hope of one's family on one's shoulders," Andrei says softly.

Paul looks at him but says nothing. I can't read his expression in the shadows.

"In my country, we have another proverb," Andrei goes on. "'Marry your son when you will, your daughter when you can.' Misha taught me that one." He smiles and looks at Paul. He leans closer. "I understand. I have a wife at home chosen by my father. She is not beautiful, but sweet, like your fiancée. And with a lot of money."

The web of half-truths and outright lies he spins wraps around Paul, light as gossamer, strong as silk, and soon the young man is confessing his plight. And yes, the hope of his family does lie on his shoulders. His is an old name and pedigree here, but there is no longer any money left. He has three sisters who need dowries.

"I am very fond of Olive," Paul says.

"Of course, you are," Andrei soothes.

The farther away we have come from the house, the closer Andrei has moved to Paul until they are now arm-in-arm. I am also arm-in-arm on his other side, but I know they have forgotten about me already. Soon Andrei will slide out from my grasp and steer Paul away from me and out of sight in the rose garden.

"A life without passion," Andrei murmurs, "is hardly worth living."

Paul is leaning into Andrei now, and I can almost feel him shiver as I withdraw into the shadows.

A woman's voice shatters the perfumed air. "Paul? Are you out here?" It's Olive, the fiancée.

I watch the two men pause, raise their heads, look at each other. Paul will be startled, pulled out of the dream he has walked into, guilt flooding over him at what he has confessed, what he has experienced.

I can almost feel Andrei's annoyance as Paul slips away from him, hurrying back to the warmth and light and security of the familiar. But he turns on the steps to the porch and says, "We'll continue our talk later, sir." He raises a hand. Even then he hesitates.

Andrei is barely visible in the shadows, and I feel him tremble with suppressed anger at the woman for her unfortunate timing. I move beside him and we watch until they finally disappear within.

"You see a wolf here, do you? An animal showing its teeth?" Andrei turns on me and pulls me into the bushes.

The attack is so sudden, I am breathless, unprepared, as he reaches for me and tears off a button in his rush to pull down my trousers. I barely have time to catch hold of the tree branch to keep my balance as he flips me around and thrusts his hand between my legs, forcing them apart.

The air is cool on my bare flesh and I am shivering. But I am hot, panting for him. Even knowing I am a surrogate, I press back eagerly against him, making his entry into me all the easier. But he does nothing to ease the pain. He grunts, thrusts, savage in his anger at being thwarted. I try not to cry out in the rose-scented night air when he comes, when I come shortly after and collapse on the cold ground. My eyes close and I begin to shake. In the pale light, my bare skin looks paper-white and sickly. When I look up, Andrei is gone. I scramble to my feet, anger almost overcoming me. I pull my trousers up and force myself to sit down on the bench to let my beating heart still.

∞

The lady of the house must have agonized over which room to assign to me, I think later that night. The musicians have left, most of the guests have gone home, their sleek long motorcars purring down the winding driveway and coughing a few times before turning toward the city or their own country houses nearby. The remaining gentlemen have had a glass of port and a last cigar with our host. By some careful maneuvering, Andrei ended up sitting beside Paul. Andrei was talking softly in that throaty intimate way he has, making it imperative for Paul to lean closer to hear what he was saying. The result was a picture of them talking and laughing together in the secret manner of lovers. I know this was all staged for my benefit, and for Paul's as well. It is a picture that others will remember later on, when it will be too late. Even knowing this didn't make it easier to bear. I can feel the air between them warming, pulsing in that overheated way I am so attuned to.

I made my excuses and retired early. What reason had I to stay? So here I am in my room, with that aching loneliness that is always with me when my lord is on the hunt. It has been a while now, while he looks around at New York society, waiting and watching, until he finds the right person, someone vulnerable, someone who connects with him in that special way I never understand. Once he saw that in me, wooed me and won me, stealing me away from the minor place I was to occupy at the Romanoff

Court. When I first met him, I felt it—his power, his raw sexuality—and frightened, I tried to hide. But I was already lost. Even hidden away in my tiny office, he tracked me down and took me on my desk, day after day, until he suggested I leave and move in with him in his palace by the river.

I give him everything. Why should he pursue others? The only thing I can no longer give him is novelty. Or the pleasure of the hunt.

Unable to sleep, I wander the corridors, making no sound on the deep red carpets, a shadow passing by the gilded mirrors. At the end of the corridor, I see a set of French doors opening onto what I assume is a balcony. I open the doors and walk out, curious as to what I would find spread out below.

The wide-pillared balcony looks out over a formal garden. A series of fountains runs down the middle, ending in the statue of a naked boy holding a large fish, water gurgling from its open mouth. Darkness has drained most of the color from the flowers, but the crescent moon silvers the leaves and gives the scene an otherworldly air that makes it beautifully mysterious. As I lean on the railing smoking one of Andrei's pungent Russian cigarettes, I see movement below, and as my eyes adjust to the dimness, I make out two figures seated near the fountain. I would recognize that aristocratic profile anywhere: the high forehead, the straight nose, the tilt of the chin. How long have they been out here? I know I should go back, should dismiss Paul as just another of Andrei's seductions, but something holds me there, watching, reliving other times, other similar scenes where I have been the loved one.

I see a flight of steps leading down to the garden from the end of the balcony and I glide down, my slippers making no sound in the fragrant air. From here, I am much closer to them. I can smell Andrei's cologne, almost taste the salt of his pale skin. They both have taken off their jackets and Andrei has his arm around Paul, whispering, coaxing, exciting.

"Just let go, Pavel. Follow your heart. Live what you feel now!"

"Please, I can't. This isn't me. I'm not… "

"Not what, *mon cher*? You're here. This is you. And you have a right to live your own life to the full."

Paul pulls away. "No, sir, I do not."

Andrei slides to the ground and idly toys with a flower he has plucked from between the cracks in the brick pathway. "We are like this flower," he says, looking up at Paul. "Growing where we are not to grow. It does not mean we don't have a right to grow at all, does it?"

I can see Paul smile, relax as he looks down at the beguiling face, silvered by moonlight. "But you plucked the flower. Now it's dead," he says.

Andrei laughs. "All right, so perhaps my simile is not apt. Is that the right word, simile?"

Paul nods, and one hand falls to Andrei's shoulder, almost as if by accident, as if he is not aware of it. It is such a slight gesture, but the weight of it falls through me and I slide to a sitting position, my knees weak with longing. I can feel the heat from Andrei's body transferred to Paul's hand, moving up to his heart, down to his groin.

Paul's expression shifts, and something in his whole body gives way as Andrei leans against him, rests his head in the man's lap. Paul moans and the next thing I know, they are both on the ground and Andrei holds Paul's face in his hands and kisses him. Paul falls on his neck and lets Andrei caress him, run his hands slowly under his shirt and across his chest, up over his shoulder and across his back. I see the passion on Andrei's face as he reaches down, down. His fingers must now be sliding into the warm crack between the globes of the man's ass. I see Paul stiffen.

"Oh, God," he moans, his voice barely audible, shaking with a new emotion. "Oh, please…"

He has lost the will to fight. He lets Andrei slip the shirt down over his shoulders, his bare back pale and enticing in the shadows. Andrei is half-naked himself, and the trousers slide off Paul, pooling carelessly around his ankles. Andrei is still going slowly, caressing, kissing, his hands busy where I can't see them, teasing and touching where no man has ever touched Paul before. He is gasping, pushing against Andrei as if he is drowning.

At last, Andrei coaxes him over and slides a finger inside him. Paul bucks like a frightened horse and almost cries out in protest. Andrei slows down and I see his face, tortured with the effort it takes to master his lust. I feel my own tears hot on my cheeks as my hand slips under the waistband of my silk pajamas to grasp myself, trying to share what Paul is feeling, feel Andrei next to me, holding my flesh.

When I open my eyes, Andrei has Paul in position against the fountain, his dark, brilliantined hair nearly in the burbling water as my lord enters him slowly in a long gentle stroke that makes the man whimper.

Andrei pauses, grabs Paul by the hair, rears back, and begins to fuck him, no longer able or willing to control his lust. Paul cries out in pain, both hands reaching out desperately to cling to the base of the statue to keep from falling into the water. Andrei shudders, lets out a high whinny and slides off Paul's naked body. After a moment, he reaches up and pulls the man down beside him.

"Wash your tears," Andrei says, sprinkling the young man's face with water from the fountain. "They are for your old life. Smile for me."

And unbelievably, Paul reaches over, pulls Andrei's face closer and kisses him.

I close my eyes, shudder one last time with the painful release of my seed, and collapse into the shadows on the stairs. All I want now is to crawl back to my room unseen and rage into my pillow. How does he know? How does he always know the ones who will give in? At this moment, I hate Andrei.

It is a small miracle that no one sees me as I stumble back to my room. In my anguish, I take a wrong turn and almost rush into someone else's room. At the last moment, the feel of the doorknob, the grain of the wood, something makes me pause and look about and realize my mistake. I pay attention as I hurry back the right way. I know I can't handle much more tonight.

Sleep is out of the question. I pace around my spacious chamber, pull back the drapes, look outside at the expanse of manicured lawn. Topiary shears have twisted the rows of yew into weird and frightful shapes that shift in the moonlight, casting odd shadows. I pull the drapes closed and turn on all the electric lights. The room is almost a caricature of what a stately home should have for its guests. It's as if our host has looked at pictures in old books, forgetting that we are now in a new century, with new ideas, more graceful lines, brighter colors. I smile, remembering what Andrei said when we stood together on arrival, looking around at the Victorian wallpaper, the fringed lamps, the mantle draped in its damask swag, the portraits of people who obviously were no kin to each other, no doubt bought by the lot at auction. "Appropriation of ancestors," Andrei whispers as we pass along the long portrait gallery downstairs. There is no beauty here.

I try to lie down in the fourposter bed but feel smothered by the heavy bed curtains, the piles of down pillows. I jump up again, pace, halt by the wall that separates me from my lover. Perhaps I should go to him now that he is tired of his plaything, perhaps even frustrated at having to wait.

And then I hear the murmuring voices.

I tense, every muscle locked in place. There is a door between our rooms, half hidden by a hideous bureau, and that is how I can hear them, how I recognize my beloved's voice. I would recognize him among a choir of men. My knees give way and I sink to the ground, covering my face with my hands.

Paul is in his room. In his bed. Lying beside that lean perfumed body that I adore, that I know so well, that I have licked and sucked, tasted, worshipped, given myself to, even taken in an act that is illegal, immoral and depraved in the eyes of the world. How has he lured Paul along this path so quickly? How can I ask that question? I know only too well that he is a sorcerer and I am nothing now but his creature. I lie on the bare floor, pushing myself against the wood that separates us, suffering with every moan, gasp and cry that comes to my oversensitive ears. In the overheated air, I come again, shuddering against the doorframe. But this draining explosion brings no relief.

I swing from longing to anger and back to baffled love. But as the night wears thin, a sense of utter betrayal invades my spirit that I have never felt before, or at least not for a long time. "I thought we had an agreement," I whisper to the silence. I thought only I was the one in your bed. You go out to them, you take them elsewhere, in their own homes, but not like this.

In my place.

At last, exhausted, I crawl into bed and fall asleep as the light peeps around the drapery.

∞

I awake, feeling hollowed out by emotion. I should've developed a thicker skin, I tell myself, and I slowly shave, dress. I check my gold watch, a gift from him, slip it back in my vest pocket. They are at breakfast now, I think, and I try the door separating us. It is still locked. I go next door and tap sharply. I call his name, open the door, walk in. Everything is neat, nothing out of place. No sign of clothing flung about, as is usual with Andrei.

"Andrushka?" I feel a strange prickle in my scalp as I take in the rumpled bed, the empty dresser, the Gladstone bag gone from the stand. In a rising panic, I check the drawers, the wardrobe. All empty. I rush downstairs to the huge stable area that our host has turned into a garage and look for the long hunter-green car Andrei rented.

"The Count and Mr. Paul Hastings left early this morning," some young man tells me, and I see a glint of cruel amusement in his eyes. He knows what Andrei has done. To me. To Miss Olive.

I straighten my shoulders, turn on my heel, and walk through the house to the room the family is using for breakfast. Unlike most of the rest of the place, this room has a woman's light touch. It is painted Wedgewood-blue, and white curtains flutter in the long French windows. There are no heavy drapes. No ponderous oil paintings. A series of silhouettes hang on one wall, watercolors of flowers on another

"Good morning," Mrs. Streusser says, looking up from buttering her toast. "We were wondering when our foreign guests would be down."

I look around the table. They are all here: the two daughters, the heavyset son, four of the guests who stayed overnight, and of course, Mr. Streusser, our host, sitting at the head of the table like a large toad, enjoying his latest snack of flies.

"You look unwell, sir," he says now, steadily chewing.

"We were just talking about Count Andrei. He has traveled so extensively and has such fascinating stories to tell," one of the daughters gushes. "We are so looking forward to more this morning."

"There won't be any more," I say, steadying myself with my hands on the back of my chair. "It is you who will have the stories to tell."

The young lady looks at me uncomprehending.

"Do you know where your fiancé is, Miss Streusser?" I ask, turning to her.

"He will be down shortly, I expect," she says, coloring slightly, not yet used to talking about Paul as her fiancé.

"I think you will find this is not true," I say. I grasp the chair more tightly as I feel a cold rage against all of these smug people, steadily chewing like oxen, unaware that part of their small world is about to explode in their faces.

Mrs. Streusser waves a pudgy hand." You Russian gentlemen do exaggerate so," she says, smiling broadly. "There is nothing strange about sleeping in a little on a country weekend. More plum jam, Elsa." A servant glides from the room, with a sidelong look at me as she passes.

"There is something strange this time," I say, keeping my voice even. "You will not see him again."

"What do you mean?" Mr. Streusser is glaring at me now. I look around the table and see a change has come over them all. The guests are watchful. The family looks alert. Are they afraid their carefully built effort to marry into society is about to collapse like a house of cards?

I turn my head and look right at Olive. "Your fiancé has run off with my lover."

Her face doesn't change so much as it freezes, the half-smile still in place. I can see her trying to understand what I have said, but it means nothing to her.

"He wouldn't dare even look at another woman!" Mr. Streusser explodes. "His very livelihood depends on this, and he knows it."

"It is Count Andrei he has run off with," I say softly.

Total silence descends on the table. Even the servants don't move. I feel a sense of power I haven't felt for a long time.

"Get out!" Streusser thunders, pushing back his chair with such force, it falls over.

I bow to Mrs. Streusser, who is sitting stunned, still uncomprehending, a piece of toast halfway to her mouth. I turn and go out into the hall.

Streusser, behind me, grabs my arm. "You perverted deviant! Bringing your filth into my house." He is trying not to shout but seems to have only two levels of speech—loud and louder.

"You are the one who invited the Count," I remind him quietly.

He rushes upstairs, pulling me with him into Paul's bedroom. I have already been here. I know it is empty. Streusser bellows like a baffled animal. Next, he rushes me down to the garage. Andrei's motorcar is still gone.

He pushes me away. ""Get out!" he shouts at me. "Out of my house, you…you sodomite!"

For a moment, I feel panic. Then I see Paul's car and scramble inside and turn the key left in the ignition. I can feel the servants watching me, their eyes burning into my back as the Cadillac roadster purrs down the long curved road.

On the drive to the city, I consider my situation. I wonder if I will get any of my things back, or if Streusser will burn everything connected with us. The only thing I will miss is my Malacca walking stick I got from my father when I left home to travel to St. Petersburg two years ago to begin my life as a minor court official. It is the only thing I have from home, and now there will be nothing else since I have been banished forever from the family hearth. Andrei has provided for me for nearly a year. I feel bereft, betrayed, alone in a foreign country. Everything I have is connected to him.

I go to the house he has rented on Fifth Avenue and drive into the garage. Paul can pick the car up later. I slip in by the side door. I pass two of the servants, but their faces tell me nothing. I see Andrei waiting outside my dressing room.

"Did you tell them?" he asks.

"What do you think?"

"Don't be cranky."

"I told them."

"Good." Andrei grabs my hand and pulls me to him. "That'll serve those upstarts right. What is that proverb you love quoting? 'They went for wool and came home shorn.'" He kisses me. Or tries to.

I hit him. Hard.

Tears brim in his green eyes. "Mishkla," he says in a wondering, wounded tone. "You don't think I care for that one, surely? I threw him out of the car in Washington Square."

"I'm tired of being used!" I shout.

"Hush, *mon petit choux*." He pulls me against his chest. His musky smell envelopes me.

"He was only trying to help his family," I say. But my arms snake around him in spite of myself. My breath is labored, I feel as if I am almost suffocating against him.

Andrei laughs. "'The tears of strangers are only water,'" he says. His hand grabs my ass and presses me hard against his growing erection. I hear footsteps and close my eyes, not wanting to see who is passing by, witness to my shame. Andrei never sees servants. To him, they are shadows only, but I see them. I feel their contempt.

Andrei releases me suddenly and goes into the bedroom. "Come here and take your clothes off," he says.

"I'm tired. It was a long, dusty drive."

Andrei turns around and pulls off his silk robe. He is naked, bathed in sunlight, his slender limbs and long delicate feet touched by gold. His tawny hair glows like dull fire and my heart almost stops.

"I can't do this anymore," I say, but I can barely force out the words and I wonder if he even hears me. He turns to the bed, climbs up among the cushions. His pale body, almost hairless, gleams against the midnight blue velvet of the bed coverings, the pillows piled around him, gold and blue and red, like a sultan about to hold court. A hookah glimmers on the low brass table beside the bed, adding to the picture.

"You deserve a reward," he says. "Don't you agree?"

"For helping you ruin an innocent young man?"

"No one is innocent, him least of all. He was selling himself. A whore is what he was. I used him because that's what he's for. He just doesn't know it. Come here."

"If Paul is a whore, what am I?" I whisper as my shirt drops to the ground.

Andrei's hand wraps itself around his swollen flesh. "Get up here and do something useful," he growls.

Although I am nearly naked, I hesitate. "Andrushka…"

He sighs and reaches for something under the pillows. "Sometimes you're worse than any woman," he says, "and if you don't get up here in two seconds, I'll use this on your ass." He withdraws a Malacca walking stick from the cushions and brandishes it in the air.

"Mine?" I asked, incredulous.

He lunges suddenly, aiming at my cock with the thin cane.

I scream.

"You deserve that for not having more faith in me, Mishkla. I knew you probably wouldn't have a chance to take it with you and we wouldn't want to leave anything important for that pig, now would we?"

In spite of the stinging pain between my legs, I leap

onto the bed and fling myself over him. "Oh, Andrushka, I do love you!"

"Prove it," he says, forcing my head down between his legs.

The rich perfumes of his body always intoxicate me. My own pain acts like a stimulus as I swallow him, forcing down the gag reflex. Andrei arches his back as I suck and savor the salt of him, taste the thick hair at his root. When he convulses, I swallow his essence, hot and bubbling over my lips as he grabs me, pressing me to his chest.

"Oh, Mishkla. You play me so well."

"When does the fiddle pick the tune?" I ask, but he only laughs and reaches for the pipe.

Bel Canto

Bel Canto

Hoarse shouts of encouragement and savage glee echoed off the high metal walls of the gym where two males slugged it out in the smoky spotlight of the ring. Glistening with sweat, the two near-naked combatants kept pummeling each other—fast, hard punches and sudden high kicks aimed with deadly accuracy. It was obvious that the blond was hurting. A trickle of blood leaked down his face from a cut over one eye and his opponent's bound knuckles had sliced open a gash on one shoulder.

Watching, Commander Lee Zuicker worked his jaw. As the senior officer present, he had the power to stop the fight, but if he did, Miles would be furious. He was the squadron champion, and as usual, there was a lot of money riding on the outcome of this fight. But something was wrong. Zuicker looked over at the doctor, who avoided his eye.

Zuicker began shouldering his way through the crowd as the noise rose to a scream of excitement. Jubilant yells broke out. Lee couldn't make out what was happening through the wall of uniformed men until a group burst into the ring and hoisted Miles up onto their shoulders, triumphant.

"I knew he could do it!" shouted the guy beside Zuicker. "A fucking clone couldn't beat our champ!"

"He almost did," his friend shouted back. "He came this close!"

"Out of my way!" Zuicker commanded.

Instantly, both men moved aside respectfully.

Seething with anger, Lee followed the fighters back to the dressing room. By the time he got there, a powerfully built man in white was giving Miles a shoulder rub. The doctor unwrapped the fighter's hands, exposing bruised and swollen knuckles.

"Leave us," Lee said, looking at the handler. He melted out the door.

"It's not as bad as it looks, Lee," Dr. Adano said

"If I'd known, I would have put a stop to it," Zuicker said, the anger rising as he looked at his lover's battered face. "Fighting a clone, for God's sake! It should be illegal! Whose bright idea was that?"

"The admiral suggested it as a treat for the men," the doctor said. "Miles is our champion; Darvon's the clone champ. It seemed a logical—"

"A fucking stupid idea is what it is!" Lee stormed. "And I don't give a flying fuck who gave the order, I'm going to complain!"

"I wanted to do it!" Miles broke in, his words coming out a bit slurred. "I thought you'd be proud of me."

"I am," Lee said quickly. "You know that. But it's reckless to do something like this in the middle of a campaign."

Miles looked away, his pride obviously hurt almost as much as his face. Dr. Adano began spreading clear gel over the abrasions.

"I count on you to fight by my side," Lee went on, forcing his voice to sound calm, trying to make the man understand his point of view. But Miles was angry too. Angry and hurt. He refused to look at Lee.

"Fine." Lee glanced at his chronometer. "Staff meeting. I'll see you later." He hesitated, touched his lover's wrist briefly and walked out.

Lee and Miles had been paired ever since the younger man had joined the sleeper troopship *Mars* years ago. Now as he walked, Lee glanced down at the military tattoos on his arms, plainly visible through the tough clear material of his uniform. The sleeves of the officers' uniforms were transparent so that their military history was instantly visible at a glance. It was so easy to lose one's own history in this kind of life: drifting in space asleep for years, reactivated to go into battle when war broke out in some far sector of the universe. Half the time, they had no clear idea where they were. After each campaign, the horrors of battle were expunged from the soldiers' memory. Each time they were reactivated, the leaders were briefed on their own history and filled in on the present theater of war. Lee sometimes wondered how much else had been eradicated from his mind, how much of himself was really missing.

This was Lee's fifth campaign and Miles had fought by his side for three of them. Loving, loyal, quick on his feet, no one could ask for a better companion, but sometimes the younger man's need for approval was wearing. And made him take chances, like today.

As Lee strode along the grey corridor towards the meeting room, a faint echo of a song began to spiral though his mind. He paused. He had heard it three times before, but always in his sleep. The music was faint, as if the singer were far away, the voice pure, sexless, yet as enticing as a siren call. He smiled and resumed walking. Too long in space will do odd things to you, he thought, adjusting the green trim around his cuffs. He was glad he had only one more campaign before he could go back to Earth, even though Earth was a place he could barely remember.

∞

The small group around the gleaming black table looked up as Zuicker entered. They were all there, even Captain Vandermeers. She smiled, seeing his glance at his wrist chronometer.

"No worries, Commander," she said. "You're on time. We were all early. How's the injury doing?"

Lee flexed his left shoulder. The pain was just a dull reminder of the deep burns he had suffered in the last skirmish. "I've been pronounced fit," he said. "Point me at 'em."

"Steady on. The Blaviens are under a flag of truce at the moment, remember. Which brings us to our business here." She hit the small bell in front of her, bringing the meeting to order. Around the table, the five men and two women looked down expectantly as the agenda glowed into life before them from the place-screens sunken into the table. He noticed at once there was an omission.

"Captain, I don't see Miles' name on the shortlist for battle honors promotions."

"Not this time, no."

"He has saved my life twice, and he is still a sub-lieutenant. I want to know why."

"Because, in the opinion of the Inner Council, he is not ready."

"But—"

"Commander, the promotion list is not up for discussion. We're here to respond to the Blavien invitation."

"We're accepting it, I take it?" Commander Woo Chang leaned forward slightly, his button-bright eyes crinkled in smiles. It was well known that he was fascinated by the Blaviens, even though he, like the rest of them, had fought their battalions as recently as three days ago.

"Yes, we've accepted. We're to go down this afternoon at 1800 hours. They've requested Commanders Zuicker and Aluona, and Rosen will go, too, along with His Excellency Yoko Ito as spokesperson for the Alliance."

Chang's face fell. He had been prepping for this assignment for weeks, Lee knew, but Chang said nothing, only slumping back slightly in his chair.

It was clear the group had been chosen to show off their battle leaders, the ones covered in military tattoos, the ones wearing the gold braid of command on their shoulder boards. Ito was one of the three members of the Diplomatic Corps on board, so his choice was obvious, too.

"They asked for me by name?" Lee asked, looking up at the captain.

"You are well known as one of our battle leaders, Commander. Is that so surprising?"

Lee shrugged. "I'm not a diplomat," he muttered.

"We don't know much about these people," the captain went on, ignoring him. "They claim to be peace-loving, yet they're responsible for starting the war in this sector by attacking their neighbors, the Zelites, who, I gather, spring from the same stock as they do. In other words, their relatives."

"Family fights can be nasty," murmured Commander Rosen, winking at Lee. Lee looked down quickly to hide his smile. He well remembered the vicious spat he had walked in on between Rosen and his lover just a few days ago, the two men so furious they weren't even aware of the interruption.

"Exactly," the captain went on. "They're pretty good soldiers, as we have witnessed, but their society is corrupt and they prefer the life of idle luxury they're used to, even though that level of life is available only to the privileged few."

"Is it true they have a black group down there?" asked Lieutenant Anita Danner.

Rosen shrugged. "None of the soldiers we've seen have been black."

"According to our reports, black Blaviens are restricted to being entertainers," the captain said.

"Most of them are eunuchs," Chang added, eager to show off his knowledge.

"One way to keep down their numbers," said Danner bitterly.

The captain cleared her throat, glanced down at the agenda and went on.

As Lee sat there listening, the strange haunting air began to twist through his thoughts again, distracting him from the tedious details of the upcoming event. He despised such hollow displays. Everyone knew the facts already. The Alliance was alarmed at the Blaviens' sudden interest in amassing large quantities of anthrocine, a compound whose only possible use was for deep space fusion bombs and like armaments. The Blaviens claimed they were interested in the stuff only for its mystical properties, and it happened that they were running out and their neighbors had lots but refused to trade for it. For a peace-loving people, they were certainly causing a lot of devastation in their corner of the universe.

He snapped to attention when he realized the others were getting up to leave.

"I trust you found the meeting useful, Commander Zuicker," the captain remarked dryly.

"Most informative, ma'am," he replied with a slight bow.

"Charmer," muttered Rosen, slipping past. "Did you pay attention to any of it?"

"This whole palaver is a waste of time," Lee replied. "It sounds as if these people don't deserve our intervention and help."

"I bet Miles will enjoy the event," said Rosen with another wink.

"At least one of us will find it interesting," Lee said, and set off to prepare his dress uniform.

∞

As it turned out, Miles was not allowed off the ship. His face was still badly bruised, and even the strong painkillers he was on couldn't disguise that it was difficult for him to move about. This was not what the Alliance wanted the Blaviens to see. All their trooper heroes on parade must seem in tiptop shape. Lee felt his lover's absence keenly as he set off in the shuttle, but he was soon involved in the final briefing being given by the ambassador.

As the shuttle hovered over the Blaviens' Great Gathering Place, Lee watched out the portal. This was the closest he had been to the main city, even though they had been fighting these people for more than a month. At first glance, the buildings were difficult to distinguish from the reddish-purple rock outcrops that formed the harsh landscape. The houses must be built into the rock, Lee thought, and from a distance, they blended in perfectly. Wonderful camouflage.

As they walked down the gangplank into the bright sunlight, it looked as if the whole community had turned out to see the cream of the Terran troop ship. Rank after rank, tall pale men and women, their narrow heads wrapped in brightly colored material, silently watched as their alien visitors swung across the courtyard and entered the wide-open doors in lockstep, following the Blavien Herald into the huge vaulted chamber.

And then Lee heard it again. That voice. That song. Rising achingly sweet and impossibly high, it floated in his mind like a memory. But this time, he realized with a jolt, it was real. As he moved into position in front of the intricately carved stool pointed out for him by the Herald, he saw a tall, commanding figure standing with his eyes closed on a raised platform at the end of the hall. He wore a nearly transparent robe with a wide embroidered panel hanging from his waist front and back. He looked unlike anyone else there, his skin a dark lustrous black with glints of gold, his shoulders wide, his chest well-developed. His hair hung down to his shoulders in long tight ringlets gleaming with oil, and his high cheekbones flared wide and caught the light. His mouth was open as the beautiful music floated out into the air.

"It's all real," Lee murmured.

"What?" Next to him, Commander Rosen leaned over to catch his words.

Lee shook his head and stared spellbound at the singer. And then the man opened his eyes and stared right at him. The eyes were luminous, and even at this distance, the effect of the light grey color was like electricity.

"Weird-looking," Rosen said with a shiver, but Lee paid no attention. He was hypnotized, staring back as if there was no one else in the room.

"You appreciate our Singer?" The pale Blavien server placed a bowl of spicy soup before him, precisely in the middle of the small metal table. "If you wish, I can ask him to visit with you later, as one of our honored guests."

"Yes," said Lee. "I would like that."

"Since when are you such a music lover?" Rosen asked, obviously surprised at his comrade's reaction. "Should Miles be worried?"

"Don't be such an asshole," Lee snapped. He was glad when Rosen's attention turned to his own server, a blond girl with an impish smile. Lee wondered when the males and females started to cover their heads. Probably at puberty, he guessed. Except for the singer.

Speeches were made to the accompaniment of the music that poured apparently without effort from the singer. Hours passed, course after course was served on the tiny metal tables before each guest, and still the singer stood there, mouth open, back straight, motionless, pouring out his soul into the air. Lee felt the effect of him as time wore on and the song wrapped around him like a moist blanket, creeping inside his clothes, under his flesh, until he found that he was breathing with the statuesque man, holding his breath when the notes drifted almost out of range, smiling when the pace quickened or the music trilled in amusement. He felt the notes like words against his ear, whispering directly to him. And every now and then as he stared towards the platform where the man stood, he met that probing unsettling gaze and shivered expectantly.

Absently, he sampled whatever was placed before him, paying little attention to the formulaic speeches that promised so much and meant so little. The glittering scene shimmered before his eyes, but for him, the singer was at the center of things, not the High Three who held the power to sign treaties. Did they really want peace? Were they willing to make the necessary concessions? Perhaps they had underrated the Terran troopers.

Lee was just slaking his thrust with a sample of the bitter-sweet wine when he felt suddenly dizzy. He looked up to see the singer sway, reach out as if blind and then slowly swoon to the floor. At once, the High Three stood up, turned as one and left the room. Feeling an unaccustomed panic, Lee jumped to his feet, too, but now the singer was surrounded and being carefully lifted up on a sort of litter and carried away almost reverently, it seemed, out of the hall.

"What the fuck?" Rosen laughed. "Guess that's why they don't make 'em fight. No stamina."

Lee gazed after the procession, his breath coming in short gasps. He felt a shuddering sense of loss, of helplessness. He had never felt like this on the battlefield or behind the sights of his Arrow GT6000. Vulnerable, he thought. I feel naked and vulnerable.

"You okay?" Rosen asked. "You're white as a sheet!"

"Of course, I'm okay!" Lee snarled. "A little indigestion." He forced himself to sit down again, suddenly aware that others had remarked on his strange behavior. He was a Hero of an Alliance troop ship. He had no right to react in a personal way to a man he hadn't even met.

The ritual meal dragged on as if nothing at all had happened, but somehow, Lee knew there would be nothing of note decided this day and he was not surprised when the Terran group was ushered back to their ship after the ordeal was finally over.

∞

In the debriefing room, Lee felt strangely exhausted. It was all he could do to concentrate on the ambassador's words.

"It appears that our intel is not very thorough," Ito remarked acidly. "Nowhere does it hint at the importance of these entertainers."

"Excuse me, Excellency," Chan broke in, "but they're more than entertainers."

"So you say, Commander, but you can't tell us how, or what they really do represent to these people. Tonight, we witnessed the fact that once that caterwauling eunuch passed out, it was game over for them. But why?"

Various suggestions were put forward, each one more foolish than the last in Lee's opinion, but no one could figure it out.

"Lee, what's your theory?" the captain asked. "I hear you were enthralled by the performance."

"I think that's too strong a word, ma'am. Impressed, yes."

"He made eye contact with you and no one else," Rosen volunteered. "Maybe you should try to get close to him and find out how this works."

"Why is it important?" Lee asked. "The singer has nothing to do with the treaty."

"As far as we know. But if he keeps keeling over and the High Three take off, the treaty may never be signed."

"The singer might be viewed sort of like a talisman to the High Three," Chan suggested. "So he has to be there to bring them luck."

Rosen laughed. "Now that sounds ridic—"

"Good!" exclaimed the captain. "That's a viable explanation, given their love of ritual and claims of mystical powers for anthrocine."

"Sounds right on," Rosen amended.

"But it's still just speculation. We have to know where we stand. And Lee's the only one he took any interest in at all. Commander, try to get close to him, to find out what hold he has over them, how it works."

"I'm a soldier, ma'am. I'm not good at this sort of thing."

"How do you know till you try, Commander? You're down there again tomorrow at 1300 hours for another go."

"Just me?"

"Just you and Commander Chang," she added, suppressing a smile. She gathered up her hat and tablet. "Good luck."

As Lee walked down the narrow corridor to his quarters, the drab colorlessness of his surroundings struck him for the first time. In contrast to the Blavien chamber where shades of red, purple, yellow and gold blended and divided and blended again, the battleship walls were uniformly grey, the ceiling a dull white. Even the floor was covered with greyish-brown carpet that did nothing at all to lift the spirit. Odd he'd never thought of this before.

He opened the door of his stark quarters and walked in, loosening his collar with one hand.

"Miles!"

His lover lay on the bed, trembling, his short blond hair darkened with sweat, his face pale under the yellowing bruises.

"I feel like shit," Miles said, his voice hoarse.

"You should be in sick bay!"

"No. It's just some twenty-four–hour thing."

"But we all had shots," Lee said, sitting down on the edge of the bed and taking Miles's hand. "You're burning up."

"I'll be fine by tomorrow," he said. "Tell me about the Blaviens."

Lee made a clumsy effort to adjust the pillows as he began to describe the Gathering Chamber, the colors, the song, the ritualized movements of the servers, the strange sour-sweet wine. Talking about it brought the while scene back in focus, made him feel again the force of the singer's luminous eyes. "I don't think they're just entertainers like we were told," he said. "It's more. Much more."

"Maybe they're prophets or something," Miles suggested. "Maybe they can see the future."

Lee smiled indulgently. "Hardly," he said, "but it's got to be something along those lines. A priest maybe?"

"Eunuchs," Miles said thoughtfully. "Why?"

"Maybe that part's wrong, too," Lee said.

"We'll get to find out tomorrow," Miles said sleepily, reaching out for his lover. "I'm glad you're not a eunuch. Lee."

But in the morning, Miles was still feverish, and a strange white rash had developed on his shoulders and across his chest and neck during the night. Lee insisted on calling in the medics who smartly carted him off to sick bay

Lee stood looking after the white-jumpsuited medics, an unusual anxiety gnawing at him. Miles was never sick. Lee wanted to stay with him, to watch over him and make sure he was being looked after properly, but it never even occurred to him to question his orders or ask to be replaced.

"Don't worry, sir," the doctor said. "Miles will be fine. I'd worry more about you, down there among the alien rocks."

Lee sighed. In the night, he had been awakened by a dim echo of the Blavien song. But this time, he recognized it for what it was, and it made him long to see the singer again. With one final look at Miles, Lee strode down the corridor to the shuttle and climbed aboard.

This time when they landed, the huge area was deserted. They were ushered inside with the same measured pomp and circumstance, but the room was smaller now, the proportions like a normal dining hall back home. Perhaps they'd added some walls, Lee thought, but he couldn't figure out where. The singer stood on his platform filling the room with his song, but the magic was gone. When Lee looked at the singer, he understood why. It was a different man. His disappointment surprised him.

As the meal dragged on, Lee's mind drifted back to Miles, wondering why a man who had never been sick should suddenly fall prey to a bug they were routinely protected against. He absently fingered the memory disk around his neck. Was there something locked inside that would tell him any different? Something that would explain that icicle of fear he had felt on finding Miles still sick this morning? On seeing that white rash?

Or were the medics right and it was only his own unpleasant memories of war recorded there? Everyone called them mem tags. And after every campaign, each soldier went through the block scan to erase the horrors of what they had been through. Everyone took mem blocker pills to keep the barriers in place. For the first time, Lee wondered what else was locked away in the sedated part of his brain. Something that might possibly help Miles?

Perhaps it was the music that had opened the door to these strange and disturbing thoughts: the song the others heard and the ghost of the one that still snaked through his brain from the other singer, the man from yesterday who had looked across the room into his soul. Somehow this was connected, he thought. He felt thick and slow, unable to grasp the delicate thread that was being spun for him. There was a pattern here somewhere, elegant and subtle like the pattern of a battle strategy spun by the generals behind closed doors.

When the meal was finally over, he was ushered into a small room where the first thing he saw was a sheet of water falling down one rippling wall into a reflecting pool. It was unsettling the silent way it fell, the way it refracted the light off the wall so that it looked as if the rock were constantly moving. Behind him, he heard the click of the locks as they slid into place. An odd ritual, but just one among many, he thought. It was only when he turned that he saw the singer from yesterday.

"I didn't mean to startle you," the man said. Even his speaking voice was musical, Lee noted, taking his time to sit down, lean back, compose himself.

"I am called Tōnidi. And you are Commander Lee Zuicker."

"Lee, please."

"As you wish."

"You weren't singing today."

"I am the First Singer. The man you heard today is the Second Singer. That is the custom."

"I guess you needed a rest," Lee said, reaching for the wine.

"Yesterday was taxing," the man admitted, leaning back and adjusting the transparent folds of his robe.

Lee looked away. "I knew an entertainer once. He used to take long holidays to recuperate."

"An entertainer?" The man gazed at Lee in evident confusion. "You think I am an entertainer?"

"I didn't mean to insult you," Lee said, cautiously.

"Perhaps I am, in the sense that you are, when you orchestrate your war games," the man went on softly.

Lee felt his spine stiffen. "That is far from entertainment," he said, his voice tight. He stopped himself from saying more, afraid he'd regret it later. This is exactly why I didn't want to do this, he thought to himself. He took a sip of wine to cover the awkward silence.

"I meant no disrespect," Tōnidi said, leaning forward. "This happens because of incomplete knowledge of each other's culture."

"I'm not a diplomat," Lee said.

"That is precisely why I contacted you."

Lee stared at the man, at those luminous eyes, such a contrast to the black burnished skin that gleamed like the sheet of moving water behind him. That song worming its way into his mind, his heart, his soul. For a reason. But why?

"I'm just a soldier," Lee said, indicating his military tattoos.

"Yes." Tōnidi sipped his wine and for a long moment there was no sound but the soft rustle of the water over the curving undulation of the wall. "We both have given up a great deal for our chosen profession," he went on, leaning forward and fixing his eyes on Lee. "You have given up family life, a settled existence with a loved one, friends outside your shipmates. And so have I. We both have our battle scars." He indicated the faint scars of surgery just visible under his high rib cage.

"I didn't know you went into battle."

"My scars are from an operation to remove two ribs in order to give me more lung power and greater range. And yes, I do go into battle, though not in the front lines. It is my voice that holds our battalions together, encourages them, tells them when to advance and when to withdraw, even though the decisions are not mine."

Stunned, Lee could only stare at the man. "I think you have given up more than I have," he said at last. Although he couldn't believe this charismatic strong man could possibly be a eunuch, he couldn't help but think that was part of what he had given up. "I have a loved one," he added. "His name is Miles Addison."

"And did you choose him?"

"Of course!"

"Really."

Lee felt that dart of anger again and forced himself to stay silent. Was the man deliberately trying to provoke him? As a means to learn something? It seemed an incompetent way to gather intel.

"I'm a plain man, Tōnidi. Tell me straight out, what do you want?"

"You are angry with me. Forgive me. Sometimes I, too, am blunt." He stretched out a hand into the water and licked his long fingers one by one. Lee watched, fascinated. "I have spent months on this campaign, just as you have," he went on. "I wanted one person on your side to understand why we need the anthrocine. Just one person of a high enough rank to have a voice. We want peace. We are not a violent people, but we will fight for what we need."

"I've had experience of that," Lee said acidly, "but the anthrocine has one purpose only."

"For you, not for us." Tōnidi got to his feet in one smooth fluid motion and reached over to touch the wall. "Put your hand beside mine," he said. After a moment's hesitation, Lee stood up and laid his own hand against the rock. "Do you feel the song?" Tōnidi asked.

"I feel vibrations," Lee said, "from the waterfall, I suppose."

Tōnidi smiled, his whole body swaying as if in time to music. Lee tried not to look at that gold-flecked muscled body so close, so clearly visible under that gauzy robe. "Our people can hear it everywhere they go. Anthrocine is a conductor. It is built into the walls of our homes and public buildings; it is woven into our clothing, mixed with the scented oils in our hair, inlaid into the patterns of our jewelry. The 'vibration' you feel is what holds us together, and your people are trying to take it away from us. Without it, we are no longer whole. What you are doing is genocide."

Lee snatched his hand away from the wall. "That's crap," he said. He checked the time again and paced over to the window, but it was too high to see outside. Uneasiness crawled under his skin like maggots. His hand tingled and his mind still heard a faint hum, like the song that had crawled through his brain so often of late. Was there a grain of truth in what the man said?

Miles, he thought suddenly. Worry about Miles is throwing me off. He turned back to face the singer.

"I know you are only doing and saying what you have been ordered to. However you see yourself, your people have been subjugated by the Blaviens. You must know what they are capable of. Why don't you join with us and be truly free?"

The singer smiled and shook his head sadly. "How do you see me?"

"A bird in a gilded cage," Lee shot back. "That's what I see."

"Because that's what you have been taught to see. But you are wrong. I *am* free, my career freely chosen and revered by my fellow Blaviens."

"Then why haven't I seen any black people here who are not singers?"

The man laughed. "Because, my alien friend, our appearance changes as a result of our specialized training and the various procedures we undergo in pursuit of excellence. Unlike the Alliance, we have no second-class citizens on our planet."

"Neither do we," Lee responded.

"And your companion? Would he agree?"

"Miles?"

"A clone. Second-class by your standards, no?"

"How dare you!" Lee glared at the singer who stared back at him calmly. Lee laughed. "Are these shock tactics something you learn in singer school? Something to give you the edge taken away by the knife? Okay, I know we have another hour and a half to go as part of your ritual after-dinner thing, but I have to check in with my ship." He walked over to the window, took out his com dev and keyed in the connection to sick bay. Behind him, he heard the soft rustle of the singer's robes as he moved away to give him privacy.

No luck. Probably too much interference, he thought, shifting a little to see if this would help. He wasn't supposed to contact the ship from a war zone but this was a truce. And he was worried. As he was about to try again, the thing buzzed in his hand. Rosen's voice, crackling with static and anxiety, came from the speaker as he held it to his ear.

"... careful! Miles just ... save him ... save..."

"What? What about Miles?"

"He's dead," said Rosen, his voice suddenly all too clear. "I don't understand it! It looks like CDS, but it can't be that! Something's going... hiding..."

"Rosen!"

But the link was gone. No matter how he tried to re-establish contact, nothing worked.

Lee stared at the device in his hand. CDS. Clone Disintegration Syndrome. Fast, deadly and painful at the end. And impossible! His mind swirled with pieces of a puzzle he hadn't even known existed. How could he find the key to make them fall into place?

He turned and looked at the man standing by the wall of water. "How did you know?" he asked softly. "How did you know about my lover?"

"I tried to contact you and sensed someone was with you. I tried to contact him, too, but... It is hard to explain."

"He was an officer," Lee went on, trying to find the logic. "Clones are created to be the privates in our army. They do most of the drudge work. The brass never promotes clones." He shivered as he remembered the briefing two days earlier when he had brought up Miles' promotion, for the second or third time. "Did you contact anyone else?"

"I tried a few of the high-ranking officers. No one responded but you. But always there was the noise, a buzz of thoughts and emotions that gave no room for me. But with...Miles, there was nothing. Well, not quite silence, but more like a faint echo of...you."

"But why?" murmured Lee, fingering the mem chip around his neck.

"There are many questions here," the singer murmured. "You said a moment ago something about *our* three-hour post-dinner locked-door conversation period. We have no such ritual. We were told it is a ritual of yours."

Lee shook his head. "No. Somebody got their wires crossed."

"Just as you were told the singers here are entertainers. That we want the anthrocine for purposes of war, that black singers are a subjugated people."

"All right, all right. Let me think." Lee turned away, leaning against the wall for a moment to collect himself. Miles, dead. Not Miles, but a clone. One thing was certain: Miles had been a soldier once, a leader who had been promoted twice. When did they do it to him? I need to know, he thought, pulling the men chip from his neck and plugging it into the com dev. Painful or not, I need to know!

As he watched the small screen, image after image flowed by, going backwards in time: violence, bloodshed, screams of pain as men were torn apart, a child crying for its mother, fireballs rolling through a village, exploding everything in their path, a starship burning with its crew still on board. All on his orders. Must have been the last campaign.

And then ... Miles ... covered with blood, delirious and screaming with pain. Miles, his face contorted in agony, looking up at him, begging for death. Lee's hand holding the gun ... Miles, his eyes clouding with death. Numbly, Lee kept watching as the images of war flowed on, back to the third campaign, and then... Miles again, dying in his arms, his cheeks and neck covered with that deadly white rash!

"Fucking Christ," he breathed, watching. With an effort, he unplugged the mem chip. "Why did they do it? Why was it necessary to defile the man's memory like this? To make a mockery of his valiant career?"

"You must be very important to them," murmured the singer. "They were willing to go to any lengths to keep you happy."

"Yeah, I'm just about ecstatic now." Lee paced back and forth, covering the length of the room quickly in his agitation, turning abruptly on his heel. Pacing back. And I loved him. The man, the clone. And just when had Miles the man died and Miles the clone taken over? How many times had he died? I loved them both the same, he thought. And that shocked him more than anything else.

With an effort, he forced himself to think of the other implications of his situation. Why he was here with this alien male. He paused and looked at the singer, who stood motionless, watching him with those luminous all-seeing eyes. He switched on the com dev again, keying in the ship's call numbers. This time, there was nothing at all. All service had been cut. It had been a fluke that Rosen got through to him at all, he realized.

And suddenly his brain snapped back into campaign mode and he saw it all. A map of treachery unfolding with the precision of an oiled machine.

He glanced at his chronometer. Just over an hour left. "Listen carefully," he said. "This situation is a set-up. I'm one of the sacrifice pawns, and so are you."

"Pawns? Is that not in a game?"

"A deadly game. Just listen. I'm an Alliance commander and I know how they operate. What I see here is the final stages of Campaign Four, which I was not intended to survive. Afterwards, they would have killed Miles anyway," he added bitterly. "But I digress. This is a classic Double Three Sacrifice Maneuver, straight from the textbook I helped write. But I never expected to be the one sacrificed."

"I do not understand."

"My people fight to win," Lee said. "They're empire builders. You fight to get what you need. We fight to control." He paused, trying to simplify his thoughts so he could get the idea across quickly. "Can you contact your people? Is that part of your gift?"

The singer smiled. "I contacted you, didn't I?"

"Yeah, and I had no idea what it meant. I mean, can you tell them something specific, like evacuate the city?"

Tōnidi stilled, looking at Lee calmly, his eyes probing for the truth. "Tell me what to say and why."

"They're going to attack," Lee said, not even realizing that by switching pronouns he had switched sides. "They never intended to talk peace. They'll attack and then take what they want and leave you broken. They sent me because you think I'm important to them, so it'll never occur to you to be on guard. Obviously, I no longer am.

They have other leaders, all eager to take my place. As for Chang, he asked questions. You have to get your people out of here. Can you do it?"

"Where should they go that your people will not follow?"

"Look, they'll hit this city hard and fast, and no one here will survive. I gather you have escape tunnels. We know about them, but not where they go. Move your people! Now! Someone will escape!"

"I will call them to unlock the door for you," Tōnidi said.

"Why?" Lee sat down and poured more wine. "Don't waste any more time."

Tōnidi moved over beside him and laid a hand on his arm. "You are a good man," he said.

"Yeah. A real peach," said Lee. He let himself touch the singer's hand for a moment, feeling the strength and the warmth, the life coursing through him. If things were different... He pulled his hand away.

Tōnidi walked over to the wall of water and bowed his head for a moment. Then the room was suddenly filled with his voice, sliding up and out beyond the walls with purity and strength. Lee sat still, listening. He couldn't read the message, but he knew what it said. From outside, he heard the sudden burst of alarm, the sound of running feet. It was their Family Day. Everyone would be at home, right where the Alliance wanted them. But now they heard their First Singer's voice and responded without question, heading for the tunnels.

Lee sat listening and drinking wine. Behind him, he heard the click of the locks sliding open. He was touched that someone had thought of them, but it made no difference. He remained where he was, watching the rise and fall of Tōnidi's chest as his magnificent voice reached out to his people. After a while, the tall man seemed to sway and stagger back. Lee jumped up and went to him at once, putting his arms around the man, who hesitated only a moment before raising his voice once more, leaning into Lee, gaining strength from the contact.

And then it happened. The building shuddered as the first shells hit the city. The glass in the window shattered. The room rocked and bits of bricks and plaster fell from the ceiling. Outside, the air grew thick with the smells of burning and explosives, a smell as familiar to Lee as breathing. He knew what would happen next, and his arms tightened around the singer, pulling the man against him as if his thick soldier's body could protect the singer from the violence around them.

And then the song stopped. "Let go," murmured Tōnidi. "All we can do now is let go."

"I'm not letting go of you," Lee said, sinking to the ground and bringing the singer with him. "Can you tell if anyone got away?"

"The Second Singer, who will carry on. Some of the families, some of the battalions who were not home. But many did not," he added, his voice now faint on the smoke-filled air.

Lee could feel the man's heart beating against his. For a wild moment, he thought maybe there might be a chance. On impulse, he bent over and kissed the man's warm dark neck under the scented curls. The man turned his head and looked into Lee's eyes. The room exploded around them.

Chops and the Stiff
by Kyle Stone

From the erotic mystery anthology *Noirotica*,
Masquerade Books, 1996

Chops and the Stiff

I was banging the kid's ass when I saw the body fall past my window. I live in a converted warehouse. The windows are big. The kid under me howled in ecstasy. I screamed. But I kept right on plowing him, riding faster and faster, as if spurred on by that glimpse of Andy "The Handyman" Maguire falling to his doom. The kid was tied to the bed but he managed to get a lot of action going, slapping his ass against my nuts and howling like a banshee in heat. His arms were stretched wide, held tight by the handcuffs that rattled against the painted metal headboard. His muscles stood out rigid like cables. His blond hair was slicked tight against his skull. His shoulders gleamed like slick marble in the light from the one naked light bulb swinging over the bed. Sometimes I like to read before going to sleep. A Walter Winchell column, maybe a story by that Parker doll. Or Damon Runyon's latest, just to see if I recognized anyone.

Tonight my bedtime story was a kid named Tony "The Angel" Sanducci. He looked like a choirboy but the only singing he did was in a customer's bed. This time, he was doing a freebie, a thank you to me for taking him in on a slow night. Outside it was as cold as a witch's tit. I had spied him under his usual lamppost outside the YMCA as I walked home from my gig playing clarinet at The Pit, lugging my axe in my arms to keep warm. One look was all it took to get him trotting at my heels all the way home.

So now the Angel was paying me back. In spades.

I came like Old Faithful on a really good day. I collapsed on the kid's muscular back, gasping and panting. I reached for a Philip Morris.

"You should lay off the nicotine and booze for a while, Chops," the Angel said.

"You should shut up." I smacked him on the ass. He grinned appreciatively. I thought of ambling over to the window to check on the status of Handy Maguire, my erstwhile upstairs neighbor, but I figured by now he was a goner, so what was the point? My apartment is a walk-up, but like I said, it's a converted warehouse with high ceilings. I'm on the fourth floor. The Handyman lives on the floor above me. Used to, that is. No way he was breathing. A police siren wailed in the night, coming closer. The Angel licked my ear. I forgot about the Handyman.

The next day, I was in the office suite I share with Cuddles LaJoya, the insurance investigator. To be more precise, I rent the broom closet she calls the second office at an exorbitant fee and we share a secretary, a little doll by the name of Hettie Gable. Her boyfriend made the whole deal worthwhile. Anyways, it was Friday and Hettie and the matinee idol had already jumped into the jalopy and headed out of town for the weekend. Cuddles was leaving early, too, with her girlfriend, and I could still hear the shouting that passed for conversation between them all the way up the stairwell.

I was just thinking about maybe hitting the road myself when the door opened and Rudolph Valentino walked in.

Actually, this citizen was a whole heap better-looking than old Rudy ever was, except that his gorgeous velvet brown eyes were red and puffy and he looked as if he'd lost his dog. Or maybe his best friend.

"I need help," he said.

Anything. I cleared my throat. "What seems to be the problem?" I leaned back on my squeaky chair and tucked my thumbs into my vest pockets.

"It's... my uncle." He folded all six feet of elegance into the chair opposite me and flung his brown fedora onto my cluttered desk. He pulled a pack of Philip Morris out of his jacket pocket and lit up with a shaking hand. A diamond pinky ring caught the light and winked at me. I almost winked back.

I was smoking one of Cuddles' cigarillos. I flicked off the ash and waited for him to collect his thoughts. My own thoughts roamed over the elegant body hiding under the Savile Row suit. It was an effort to concentrate.

"My uncle died yesterday. The police say he... that he killed himself... jumped out of the window in his apartment on the fifth floor. They say—" He stopped and took a long drag on his cigarette.

I sat up abruptly and began to pay more attention. This citizen did not look like any relative of the Handyman. On the other hand, he wasn't paying me to think about family trees. On the third hand, he wasn't paying me. Yet.

"They say he left a note."

"I'm very sorry for your loss," I said, "but I don't see what I can do for you."

"It wasn't suicide!"

"If he left a note, then I don't see how you can argue—"

"I don't care about the note. It's not possible, that's all!" He stubbed out his cigarette fiercely, as if trying to annihilate the thing from the face of the earth. He was one unhappy citizen. And he had wonderful strong-looking hands.

"Look, ah... I don't think I caught the name."

He raised his head and looked me square in the eye and I saw the thoughts roll through his head as plain as if he was talking out loud. He was going to lie. Then he changed his mind.

"I'm Alistair Cunningham III," he said. "I can pay you handsomely."

"For what?"

"To find out what happened."

His eyes were a melting brown (did I mention that?) and they were so deep I knew if I dived in, I might never get out again. I didn't care. I'm a sucker for brown eyes. And besides, I need to eat, like the next guy.

"My name's D.D. Domingo, but my friends call me Chops."

"I know. You're a jazz musician part-time. You play clarinet with the Dixie Cups at the Pit on Thursday nights."

"This is about Handy, isn't it?" I said. "And he's not your uncle."

Alistair Cunningham III turned a lovely shade of magenta. I hurried on. "Don't worry, I'm the last person who'd try to shake you down. I knew Handy had someone, but he wouldn't talk. Made me wonder."

"Now you know."

Swell. Somehow the knowledge didn't make me feel any better about the whole thing.

"How about we mosey on over to Luigi's Diner on the corner and you can tell me what you think I can do for you," I said, reaching for my hat.

"Diner?" he said.

"The back room," I said. I winked. It was worth it just to see that wonderful blush creep up to the roots of his hair.

The back room at Luigi's was by invitation only. The tables there were far apart, with checkered cloths and candles for atmosphere and homemade chianti flowing like water. The chef, a guy named Chris, wore a blond wig and lipstick and on special occasions, a dress. It took a while for Alistair to relax, but when he did, his story flowed out of him all in one piece.

It seems our boy had been going with Andy for about a month. It was all very hush-hush, with Alistair renting a suite at the Metropole under a false name and Andy sneaking in by a side entrance. I couldn't picture it myself, Alistair not being the sneaking-around type, know what I mean? Who can figure such things? So it turns out Alistair had just talked Andy into letting him rent a classy pad in the village for the two of them where they could live as uncle and nephew.

I took another belt of vodka straight up and told him it didn't make no sense to me. Who could think about such things as suicide with a looker like this waiting for you at home? Not to mention paying the bills.

"He was going to keep his place in the warehouse to use as a workshop," Alistair said, his voice wobbly. "He loved fixing things, you know. He was so creative that way." He pulled out his linen handkerchief and blew his nose. "He was worried about something, too."

"Like?"

He shrugged elegant shoulders. I poured him more wine. I remembered all those late nights, with Handy bumping up the stairs with yet another piece of old junk he found making his rounds in the wee small hours. He could fix anything, have it working good as new or better in a few hours, like as not. And he could refinish wood and patch up any old dresser or what not, sell it as a genuine antique down in the market. A real loss to society in my books.

My companion had given up all pretense of the stiff upper lip. He was bawling like a baby, what with too much wine and sympathy and all. There was no getting any more info out of him tonight. What could I do but take him home?

Apparently, booze made the kid horny as hell. I was always horny, so there was no problem there. We fell on each other right there on the couch before we even got to the bed. I pulled off his trousers and pried him out of his boxers in no time at all. His equipment was as fine and elegant as the rest of him: none too long, perhaps, but pretty and anxious to please, rearing up straight from his belly and pointing at me. I gulped him down and suckled on him and drank his sweet milk like there was no tomorrow while he lay back, his dark head tumbled back off the couch, his hair hanging down in sweat-drenched locks as he bucked and moaned and carried on. When he came the second time, he cried.

Then I flung him over on his stomach. He was limp as a rag doll, exhausted yet aching to be used as Andy had no doubt used him. I fucked his pretty pink dimpled ass. As I bucked and thumped into him, I glanced at the window and almost lost it. The light was just the same. I was pumping ass just the same. My mind began playing tricks on me, and I almost saw the Handyman's body fall past the glass, only this time in slow motion, giving me and him time to look at each other. My heart raced. I came.

I lay on the guy's back, catching my breath, my mind turning over like an eight-cylinder engine on high octane.

"Have you got a key?" I said at last.

He looked at me, his face tear-stained. The brown eyes were luminous and sated. "Key?"

I jerked my head towards the ceiling. "Andy's place," I said.

He hiccupped a little and began to sit up and pull himself together. His face was pale now, the sexual heat fading. "No. We always met at the Metropole. Why?"

"I want to take a look around up there. If it was murder, we might find out the reason."

He looked about to lose it again, so I pulled him into the shower and turned on the water full force. It took longer than usual to get clean, seeing as how I kept being turned on by the guy and he kept wanting to suck me off. Finally, the hot water gave out and so did we.

Dressed again, I armed myself with my trusty John Roscoe; my 'tool kit', a gift from a sexy second-story man of my acquaintance; and a flashlight and we started up the stairs. Half way up, the timed light went out, as per usual. Alistair grabbed my arm. He was trembling. I flicked on the flashlight.

There was yellow crime scene tape over the door to Andy's place. I peeled it off carefully and tackled the locks. There were three of them, but none was much of a challenge. I caught Alistair's hand as he reached for the light.

"The cops might have a watch on this place outside," I hissed. "Cool it with the lights."

We went inside and closed the door behind us. Just like my place, there were no curtains on the windows. The dull orange night of a big city that never sleeps seeped in, casting a strange pall over Andy's possessions. Like my place, too, the whole apartment was one open space. Junk was everywhere, piled in heaps, leaning against the walls, even hanging from the ceiling. Bicycles were chained to one wall. Wooden tea boxes were stacked against another. In one corner, a workbench was set up, tools neatly lined up in place over a huge chest holding nails and different grades of sandpaper, small cans of refinishing stain and paint chips and bottles and rags. It was ordered chaos.

"It's hopeless," Alistair said. "How can you find anything here?"

"It would help if I knew what I was looking for," I said. I ran my hand over a small table Andy had apparently been working on. The top was smooth as satin. There were two flaps that you could put up on either side to make the thing bigger and a small drawer in the middle. The drawer was missing.

"Looks like a desk over there." Alistair went over to the window and started going through the drawers.

Junk, I thought. Junk that the Handyman turned into treasure. But was it valuable enough to kill for? Or had the kid who was going through his desk right now been telling the truth, the whole truth and nothing but the truth?

"Someone's coming!"

We got out of there like greased lightning just as a couple of cops began thumping up the stairs. They paused to light up, giving us time to slip into my place.

And out of our clothes.

The next morning, Alistair was gone and there was an envelope with five Cs inside on my coffee table. Now I knew how the Angel must feel after a swell night with a client with bucks. Except Alistair was supposed to be the client here, not me. I pocketed the C notes and decided not to think about it.

∞

"We gotta stop meeting like this," I said to Cuddles LaJoya on the stairs outside our office.

"I'd be happy if we stopped meeting entirely," she snapped.

"Guess who hasn't had her java?" I said.

She grunted and disappeared into her office. "If you want some, come on in," she said over her shoulder. I did.

"Take a load off," Cuddles went on, handing me a mug of steaming ink. Hettie had a way with coffee no one else had. Or wanted. Still, the stuff was useful to jumpstart the morning.

We chatted about this and that and then I told her about Alistair III. I told her most of it, leaving out a few of the C notes, which was just as well because next thing I know, she's holding out her hand and mentioning the tab I was running up for the rent. I handed over one of the notes, which seemed to satisfy her.

"So what do you know about lover boy?" she asked, getting down to detecting.

I guessed right off she didn't want to know about his dimpled ass, so I told her the stuff he'd told me about him and Andy.

"And you believe it?" she said, stabbing the air with her cigarillo.

"Sure," I said. It sounded lame, even to me. Cuddles was pushing the wrong buttons, so I picked up the java and made for my own broom closet, waving to Hedda en route.

By the afternoon, I knew a lot more about Alistair. I found out he'd been expelled from Princeton on some nebulous grounds. It didn't take a genius to figure that one out: seemed he was always around this Reggie Harris, and they both belonged to the same sailing club. When I phoned Alistair to ask about Reggie, he sputtered and stammered and I could just imagine the magenta blush rushing over his face.

"That was before I met Andy," he said at last. "And aren't you supposed to be investigating Andy's death rather than snooping about in my business? That's what I'm paying you for, remember."

Properly reproved, I started dialing again. This time, I found out Andy was a bit more of a horseplayer than I'd realized, but none of the bookies holding his markers were carrying all that much action. On the other hand, someone had recently bought up said markers. Someone big. Finally, I found Mooch Munro in Kelly's Place and he whispered the name Lucky Mariano. It didn't make sense. I decided to go home and give the matter some serious thought.

Practically outside my building, I ran into Tony "The Angel" Sanducci looking pinched and hungry. He had a black eye and a split lip.

"That door you walk into have a name?" I asked.

He shrugged. "Cost of doing business," he said.

That made me mad, but there was nothing I could do about it. When I invited him inside for a little first aid and a drink, he didn't argue.

My place was looking pretty scruffy, too, what with the bed still unmade and dust lying thick on every surface. The Angel didn't seem to notice. He cleaned himself up and plopped down in my one armchair. Just about to put his feet on the coffee table, he stopped.

"Well, well. You're keeping some pretty dangerous company lately, I see, Chops." He was staring at Alistair's calling card that had been in the envelope with the C notes.

"A client," I said, "with killer eyes."

"And a killer boyfriend," the Angel said. I stared at him. "You don't know? That's Lucky Mariano's new boy, Al the Gent."

I shook my head in astonishment at this news. It took the Angel a full five minutes to convince me, along with the information that Al the Gent had picked him up a week ago and pumped his ass while the boyfriend pumped him for info about me.

"Well, I'll be damned," I said.

He agreed that I probably already was, considering the circumstances.

"He went to all that trouble just to get inside Andy's place? But why? They could have just broken in and trashed the place."

"Guess I gave the impression you two you were more pally then you were."

"Swell."

"Better we should check upstairs again," Tony suggested.

I nodded. I was remembering Alistair's interest in Andy's desk, and within minutes, we were inside, checking through the papers it contained. Nothing.

Then my eye caught the table Andy had been working on, the one with the missing drawer. With something to look for, it took us a mere twenty-five minutes to come up with it nestled inside a cabinet with a busted door.

"There's nothing here," the Angel pointed out, turning the drawer upside down.

Disappointed, we decided to give up since we had no idea what we were searching for.

I invited the Angel to come with me to the club for some dinner and for me to pick up my mail from Max. I found an envelope addressed to me in Andy's handwriting. Inside was a long flat key and a card with the words: "Stash this for me, please. I'll pick it up later. Thanks," Andy had scrawled on it.

"Weird-looking key," the Angel remarked.

"It's for a safety deposit box. Come on. I gotta make some phone calls." I headed to my usual table.

It was pretty early for the guys who hang out at the Pit, but Max set us up with Reuben sandwiches, a plate of pickles and a telephone and left us alone. I called my favorite copper, Teddy "The Bear" Robinson, and told him about the matter.

"We never bought that suicide note," Teddy growled. "Figured it was bad debts, though. This sounds more in'eresting."

"If you can be at The Pit around eleven tonight, I can guarantee you an interesting time," I said.

There was a pause. "As long as you're not playin'," he said and hung up.

Then I called Alistair. It took some doing to talk him into it without mentioning the key, but I finally got him to agree to drop in around eleven tonight.

"This I gotta see," the Angel said. His eyes were so bright, it sent shivers down my spine.

"If you're here, it'll blow the whole thing," I pointed out. He pouted.

Then I told him about the small area backstage where

the guys stash their stuff before a gig. "You can watch from there," I said, "but stay out of sight."

By the time Alistair arrived just after eleven, the Angel was nowhere to be seen and the Bear was behind the bar with Max cleaning glasses, with a stogie rammed in the corner of his mouth. Two other citizens who were probably cops sat sullenly at a table in one corner. A few even more unhappy-looking customers held down another table by the bar. Apart from that, it was the usual crowd.

I showed Alistair the envelope with the key, and the sullen individuals by the bar were all over me. Alistair changed before my eyes into Bugs Moran, heater and all.

"Get it, boys!" he said.

"You disappoint me," I managed, just before a fist slammed into my kisser.

It was all over by the time I came to. The Angel was leaning over me, holding my head in his lap and crying real tears.

"It's okay, kid," I assured him, rubbing my jaw. "Just help me get back to my place."

"They took the Gent and a couple of Lucky's hoods down to the local slammer," the Angel told me. "The whole thing's to do with some extra set of books the Handyman found in that table he was fixing up."

"All he wanted to do was turn junk into antiques," I said, one arm around the kid's strong shoulders. "Guess he couldn't resist a little more larceny."

"Know what I can't resist?" the Angel smirked. "A good tool. Always turns me on. Especially when used by a good private dick."

Somehow I was feeling better already as we lurched up the stairs to my place and tumbled in the door, heading for the bed.

This time, I made sure I wasn't facing the damn window.

The Secret Child

The Secret Child

"It doesn't look like much, does it?" Eulio remarked, looking out the window of their shuttle as it was about to land on the Subarian Colony.

Triani peered over his shoulder at the jumble of grey buildings, squat and ugly in the smoke-filled air. "Holy shit! If I didn't need the credits, I'd tell the ship to head home right now!"

"It's too late for that." Eulio sighed. "I don't know why I let you talk me into this."

"You were bored." Triani stared down at the huddled sooty buildings. "I think I've been here before," he said slowly.

"Why? This place isn't exactly on the main touring circuit."

"Must have been twelve, fifteen years ago. I can barely remember it. Back then, I was soloist with the Hills Company and I took every off-planet gig that came my way." He peered out the porthole again. "Now I understand why they're paying us so much."

"You know, Triani, you wouldn't be broke if you scaled down your extravagant lifestyle."

"I'm not broke!" Triani whirled to face him, hands on hips. "And I've worked my ass off for everything I have! Nothing was ever handed to *me*!"

"Look, I can't help the accident of birth that gave me a title," said Eulio wearily.

"So it was an accident that put the gold chain around *your* waist and threw *me* on the street? An accident that I'm the despised result of illegal self-insemination?"

"Nobody would know if you'd stop shouting about it!"

Triani turned abruptly and threw on his long glittering coat, a recent acquisition that had cost about as much as he paid his estate Keeper for several months. He snapped his fingers and the four Merculians who had been hovering by the door sprang to attention and began checking the floats piled high with baggage. Uncertain about their hosts' technical sophistication, they had brought everything necessary to ensure a full theatrical experience: lighting, music, sets, even their own floating floor. The Subarians would get their money's worth.

For hundreds of years, Subaria had been a Terran colony dedicated to mining a substance that was no longer valuable. The people had been bred especially for their task, resulting in a broad-shouldered, stunted race of humans well suited to their former underground life but now abandoned to their fate. They had done surprisingly well on their own in the last twenty years, but now, apparently, they longed for something beautiful. They longed for the music and dance and art they had been denied when under the thumb of their greedy masters. The hermaphrodites of Merculian were well known as the entertainers to the galaxy, and superstars Triani and his dance partner Eulio Chazin Adelantis were a natural, albeit very expensive choice.

"This air is foul," Eulio muttered as they emerged from the shuttle.

Triani coughed. "Holy shit, I can hardly breathe!" He covered his mouth with one hand as they swept down the gangplank, followed by their entourage.

A crowd of squat Subarians had come to meet them, unsettling in their complete silence. The superstars were used to cheering fans, people who called out to them, applauded as they appeared, threw them flowers and candies and sometimes other things, depending on the custom of the place. But these people had no custom, no established way to greet performers. They stood shoulder to massive shoulder and stared silently at the slight golden-skinned hermaphrodites from another glittering world, exotics dressed in clinging garments with more color than most of them had ever seen.

A male and a female detached themselves from the crowd and came forward, their flat faces expressionless. They were dressed identically in rumpled grey pants and black jackets. Their hair was a colorless brown and cut short over their prominent ears. The female wore a silver hoop in each earlobe. Triani was envious. Merculians had no external ears and Triani always wished he could decorate himself as Terrans often did.

"Welcome," said the female, bowing her head and clasping her hands in front of her. "I am Sharonelle Hugo and this is Haroldy LaMott." She gestured to the male. "It is a privilege to have you here," she went on, her voice a low monotone. "I'll show you to your rooms, if that suits."

"Certainly," said Eulio, bowing graciously.

"The quicker the better," said Triani, and coughed. "We need some sort of rehearsal space for tomorrow."

She nodded. "That's all arranged."

They followed her through the silent crowd and into the building, which looked like a series of cubes piled haphazardly on top of each other. The heavy doors swung shut with a sucking sound. At once, the air became better, but the gloom increased. Immediately, the Merculians tensed. Used to near endless daylight on their home planet, they found darkness threatening.

"Tomorrow's concerts are at one o'clock and five o'clock," Sharonelle said, oblivious of her guests' consternation. She stopped at a door recessed into the wall.

"Who else is on the program?" Triani asked.

She stared at him. "No one," she said.

"But—"

Eulio laid a restraining hand on his arm. Triani felt the warning like a scald and pulled away.

"If you wish anything to eat or drink," Sharonelle went on, "please ring this bell." She opened the door and pointed out a bellpull right inside.

"Thanks, sweetie, we ate before landing. Which is a damn good thing," he added, "since I just lost my appetite." He pushed past her into the room.

"But it was very thoughtful of you to offer," Eulio added. He smiled and followed his partner.

"The rehearsal space is down the hall, first door on your left," Sharonelle said and closed the door softly.

"They never said we were the whole show," Triani exploded.

"Well, we sent them the exact running times of everything we're doing," Eulio said, "so they must know it'll be a short program."

Triani strode around the room, turning on all the lights he could find. He discovered two doors opening into other rooms. "At least, we each have our own space," he said.

"They must have heard how you hate sharing," retorted Eulio. He checked his chronometer and took out a tiny com dev from the inside pocket of his tunic. "I'm going to try to reach Orosin and then go to bed. I'd suggest you stop bitching and get some sleep." He closed the connecting door.

"Suggest whatever you want," Triani shouted after him. "You're not my keeper."

He scowled. Everything came so easily to Eulio. Wealth, position, talent, even love. To top it all off, Eulio's name always came first on the program, and every time Triani saw the marquee, he felt a stab of envy. He opened a bottle of the Merculian mint wine he always brought with him and poured himself a glass.

He was just about to take a drink when he heard a muffled thump at the door. He ran a slim hand though his black curls and went to investigate.

A female Subarian stood there, smiling nervously. "Hello," she said. She carried a plate of sticky-looking cakes of some sort. Triani's stomach turned over. "My name's Rutheen Wilson," she went on, "and I'm your hostess for tonight."

"I don't think so," said Triani. This woman was not young, not even vaguely attractive, but it was obvious she had made an effort to make herself look her best. She wore sparkling slides in her straggly hair and had sewn red buttons down the front of her worn jacket. "It was a long trip, sweetie." He began to close the door.

"Please. I won't be long." She edged closer. Was this some sort of welcoming duty she had to perform? Was there someone else pushing themselves into Eulio's room right now? The thought made Triani grin with secret pleasure.

He stepped back. "Okay, sweetie."

She almost scurried past him in her relief, making for one of the tired orange armchairs in front of the low table. She set the cakes down and twisted her hands in her lap.

Triani already regretted letting her in. He offered her wine, which she declined. He perched on the chair opposite her, glanced pointedly at his chronometer and took a drink.

"You don't remember me, do you?" she said, shifting in her chair.

"Should I?"

"I was your hostess last time you were here."

"That was a long time ago, sweetie. I've been hundreds of places since then, met thousands of people. Sure you won't have any wine?"

She shook her head. "I was younger then," she said and laughed shakily. "You look exactly the same."

Humans age much faster than Merculians, he suddenly remembered. Perhaps she had been pretty then. Even desirable. He had a reputation for jumping anything that moved, but he did have standards. He looked at her more closely, but no dim memory stirred. "I tour a lot," he said with a shrug.

"I know. I didn't really think… Anyway, since last time I've become the Merculian authority around here."

Triani relaxed. People were always curious about them. "Sure, sweetie, ask away, but first I have a few questions of my own. Do you have many artists touring here?"

"Not really," she said. "We don't have enough money to bring companies in on a regular basis, so we vote on who we want and save up, sometimes for years."

Triani crossed his legs. He gave a fleeting thought to the astronomical fee he was charging. "It's that important to you?"

She nodded. "It's for the children," she said. "They deserve to see the best."

"So what do you want to know?" he said.

Rutheen sat up straighter, pulled a notebook out of her pocket and began.

∞

The next morning, Triani was annoyed to discover that Eulio had not been disturbed by a visit from a Subarian hostess. "They probably know I'm jeweled to Orosin," he said, checking his dance bag.

Rutheen had stayed until Triani could barely keep his eyes open, asking probing questions far beyond the usual range, straying into health issues, diet, even psychology.

She would deserve her position as the Merculian authority now, he thought.

After a quick breakfast of protein cubes, the dancers walked together down the gloomy hall to the first door on their left. It swung open with a creak, revealing a surprisingly large bright room lined with mirrors.

"What a relief," Triani said. "I didn't know what to expect."

Eulio dropped his dance bag on the ground and adjusted his slipper. "Nice mirrors." He pushed his blond hair up under his cap.

Triani sank into a deep knee bend, his back straight, his black eyes watching his image critically in the mirror. A few more stretches and bends and he was ready. With a glance at his partner, he activated the music. Right on cue, they raised their arms, arched their backs and went in perfect unison into the long complicated dance sets that formed the basis of their art.

After a few minutes, Triani stopped.

"What's the matter?" Eulio stopped too, glancing around the room.

"Someone's watching us."

"Aren't you used to that by now?" Eulio smiled, but there was a shadow of doubt in his round blue eyes.

"I don't mind people watching, but why hide?"

His partner glanced over his shoulder, then shrugged. "You're just imagining things," he said, but he didn't activate the music.

Triani touched the mirror and froze. "Holy shit!"

"What is it?" Eulio joined him, laid his hand beside his partner's. "I don't feel anything."

"Nothing, I guess. Let's keep going."

But as the music swelled around them again, Triani's mind was only partly on the routines that were as familiar to him as breath itself. Merculians were touch empaths, but he couldn't have felt through the glass what he was sure he had. It was impossible.

Half an hour later back in their rooms, Triani sank into a chair. "Someone *was* watching us," he said. "I know it."

"So what?" Eulio threw off his striped robe. "I'm going to take a shower."

Triani began to pull off his sweaty tank top and stopped. "Shit. I left my towel back there," he muttered. He paused, thinking of asking Eulio to come with him, then shrugged off his hesitation. Before he could give it any more thought, he ran lightly down the dim hall and opened the door.

Movement. Whispers. A scurrying sound. One of the mirrors hung open, a door to another room. Triani sprang forward and caught it just as it started to close. Fiercely, he pulled it open again and gazed up into the furious face of a young Subarian.

"Holy shit!" Triani stepped back. The youth had the round eyes of a Merculian but he towered over Triani. "Who the hell are you? Why were you watching us?"

"We paid for the privilege," the youth said. His words came out in a light Merculian voice, so at odds with his heavy frame.

"You pay for a seat in the theater," Triani said, "not rehearsal time."

"What do you care?"

Triani looked around and saw others there, lurking in the shadows in the hidden room. "Who *are* you?"

"Dance students." Another light Merculian voice, but this youngster looked female although she was Triani's height, unusually short for a human.

"What the hell do you care anyway?" The black-eyed youth suddenly pushed Triani back into the rehearsal room with great force and slammed the door shut.

Triani hit the floor hard. "How dare you!" he cried, outraged. He jumped to his feet and pounded on the glass. But now there wasn't even a seam to show where the door had been.

The dancer picked up his monogrammed towel and rushed back to his room to tell Eulio. But what *had* happened, he asked himself, standing in the drab room, rubbing his bruised buttock as he waited for his partner to get out of the shower. A few curious dance students had spied on them through a two-way mirror. One had lost his temper and pushed him. Two of them had light voices. What did that prove? One had eyes that, for a moment, had looked Merculian. That didn't sound like evidence of...anything. He decided not to tell his partner. What was the point? The person he wanted to talk to was Rutheen.

∞

But it seemed that Rutheen was the one person he couldn't get hold of. No matter how many times he pulled the bell in his room, no one would bring her to talk to him. Finally, as he and Eulio followed their guide through more endless dim corridors to the surprisingly well-equipped theater, he put Rutheen out of his mind and concentrated on the performance ahead.

Triani walked on stage with his usual arrogant stride, but as they worked through the technical rehearsal, he felt once again that they were being watched. He wasn't worried. That lout would surely not try anything in public. Triani always felt safe on stage.

The performance went off without a hitch. Both stars added an encore solo at the end, and for once, the Subarians seemed to come to life and applauded lustily. Triani found he was counting the hours before they could leave, head back home where everyone knew who he was and no one would dream of pushing him. All he wanted now was to forget this place and never come back.

After the incident with the lout, he had made it clear he wouldn't see anyone after the show. As a rule, he loved to meet his admirers, to feed off their adulation as he gradually came down from the performance high, but something here was eating away at him and he couldn't figure out what it was.

Someone knocked timidly at his dressing room door. Not a Merculian obviously. Triani frowned. Who was ignoring his orders?

"It's Rutheen Wilson," came a voice from the other side of the door.

Triani sighed and got to his feet. His former desire to question her was gone. All he wanted now was to forget the whole thing and go home.

"I won't answer any more questions," he said, opening the door.

She stood there, clutching a bedraggled bouquet of sooty flowers. He took them gingerly. The smell of chemicals clung to them, obscuring any natural scent they may once have had.

"I'm so, so sorry," she said. Her eyes were brimming with tears.

Surprised, Triani stepped back and invited her in. He had been expecting the usual sort of gushing compliments about the performance. Without a word, he opened the Merculian mint wine and poured two glasses. This time, she took one.

"What are you sorry about?" he said, curling up on the big chair. He wished he had a tranq stick with him.

She sat on the dressing table stool and took a drink. "The children have been looking forward to this ever since we finalized the details," she began. "But they were forbidden to contact you directly. It was an accident that you met them."

"Children? You're joking, right?"

"They're just teenagers."

"Is that lout who attacked me dangerous?"

"Kellan is my child," she said. "And yours."

Triani laughed. "What kind of con are you trying to run on me?" he asked. "You're not the first one to try it, sweetie. That's why I've got the best lawyers in the galaxy."

"It's not a con," she said, her voice trembling. "It was an accident. We have trouble conceiving, thanks to what has been done to us for generations: the chemicals in the air and other things you don't need to know. So about fifteen years ago, we began to take fertility drugs. It was an experiment. When you came, we knew how you looked at sex as...well, a recreational activity, so the Council sent some of us women to be with you. There were eight of you here. Six of us conceived."

Triani reached for his bag and rummaged around for a buzzer. This didn't sound like the usual con. He remembered the round Merculian eyes in the lout's face, the anger he had felt in the touch, the unsettling familiarity.

"I'm not buying it," he said unsteadily.

"We could prove it easily," she said, "but we don't have to. It doesn't matter. I wasn't even going to tell you but then this happened, and... I didn't know what you might do. I've heard about Merculian being possessive of its citizens, even half-breeds. We don't want to lose our children. Especially now."

She was holding the glass so tightly, Triani thought it might shatter. Automatically, he got up and refilled it along with his own. He drank the whole thing in silence and filled it again. "Look, we Merculians know how to prevent pregnancies."

"It was the fertility drugs," she said. "We didn't take any precautions because we were trying to conceive. With our men, I mean. It didn't occur to us—"

"That hermaphrodites were so potent?" She blushed. "It wasn't working out with your males, was it? So you slept with us. Many times, eh, sweetie? We certainly wouldn't turn you down."

"*You* certainly didn't," she said, "though one or two of you preferred the males who worked backstage."

"Most of us don't care, one way or the other," Triani said, wearily. "Look, I'm not at fault here. I take no responsibility. You say it was the drugs you were on, fine. It's not my fault."

"Stop talking about fault!" she exclaimed. "The children are a gift!"

"So what do you want from me?"

"I just thought you deserved an explanation. I thought you might figure it out or come asking questions. I heard you wanted to talk to me, and I thought that was why. They're upset about it, too," she added.

"They? How many are there?"

"Five, but two died."

"Not very good drugs if you only got five kids from eight Merculians." He laughed, the sound harsh in the bare room.

"You and I had five," she said. "The whole group numbers twenty-three."

Triani nearly dropped his glass. "Excuse me," he said after a moment. He got up and went through to Eulio's dressing room, found a buzzer in his partner's dance bag and popped it in his mouth. Back in his own room, he waited a minute as the outer layer dissolved on his tongue, sending the welcome melting feeling though his bones. He took a deep breath. "So let me get this straight," he said, sitting down again. "You say I have three children here, and one of them is the lout who attacked me."

"Stop calling him that. His name is Kellan Wilson. He's the only true hermaphrodite in the group, incidentally. The other two...didn't make it."

"Holy shit."

"A number of the children are dying, actually," she said. Her voice was so faint, he wasn't sure he had heard her right.

"Dying? Why?"

"It's the air. It's better than it used to be, but we can't completely stop the poison gasses from leaking out of the underground caves. The rock here is very porous. We're pretty much immune to it, but apparently, Merculians have delicate lungs. Over time, some of the children became susceptible to the pollution. That's why we put in the air lock doors and the new indoor air purifiers. But it's not enough. We can't afford air-scrubbers for only twenty-three people. It's too late now, anyway."

"Look, sweetie, wouldn't it be more to the point to spend your credits bringing in medical experts rather than dancers?"

"We did. Nothing can be done. Kellan and the others, they wanted to see you dance in person. That's why we've done this. It's the only thing they've ever asked for."

"Kellan didn't seem all that glad to see me."

"He has a temper. And he's very frustrated. He has the urge to dance, the creativity and talent, but he inherited my physique. Pretty hard to be graceful with my shape."

My child, Triani thought. Locked in an awkward body, longing to fly. He felt his throat close and turned away, blinking back tears. "And the other two?"

"One girl, one boy. Well, he's a boy now. He had to have a minor operation."

"And they're...sick?"

"I told you! Our children are dying."

Triani stood up. "I want to see them," he said.

She smiled bitterly. "You may be a superstar, *Chai* Triani, but you're not a miracle-worker. What good can it do?"

"They're my children, you say. I want to see them. Isn't that natural? Or do Terrans not give a damn about their offspring?"

"I didn't expect you to be paternal, that's all."

"Look, sweetie, you don't know a damn thing about me and how I feel about things." He began to pace. "Did it ever enter your tiny mind that if you'd contacted me a lot earlier, we might have saved them? Maybe they needed Merculian medicine. I have influence, don't you understand? I know everyone!"

"We didn't think you'd care."

"Holy shit!"

"You might have taken them away, and we couldn't allow that."

"So you played god with my children's lives? And now you'll lose them anyway!"

Rutheen got to her feet. "You think we didn't bring experts here?" she said, her voice vibrating with anger. "You think we're stupid as well as poor?"

Triani backed up. "Okay, sweetie, calm down. I apologize. Just back off!"

Rutheen stopped and looked down at him, her face a mask again.

"Look, I just want to see them, okay? We didn't part on the best of terms," he added wryly.

There was silence in the dressing room for several seconds. "I'll ask them," she said, turning away. "If they agree, we'll meet you in the rehearsal hall half an hour after the final performance."

She opened the door and went out, closing it softly behind her.

∞

The theater erupted in applause. "That's more like it," murmured Eulio, as they took their bows center stage. They bowed again, then withdrew one final time.

Triani grabbed a towel from the stagehand waiting in the wings and wiped his sweating face and chest.

"What were you trying to prove out there?," Eulio said, releasing his long damp hair from the jeweled cap. "I thought you were coasting this time."

"I don't coast," Triani snapped, marching down the corridor to his dressing room ahead of his partner.

"Okay, but you never add a totally new number to the program as a second encore either. I thought the stage crew would have heart attacks."

"They didn't. It worked. What's your fucking problem?"

"Don't be so vulgar! I was just wondering why the sudden—"

Triani whirled on him. "Eulio, drop it! Just...drop it."

Eulio opened his mouth, then instead, reached out to touch his hand. "Whoa. What happened?"

Triani pulled away. "I can't talk about it now. I have to meet some... people."

"We're out of this cursed place in three hours," Eulio reminded him.

"I'm not liable to forget that, sweetie," growled Triani. Eulio slammed his door.

Triani found he was shaking as he took off his makeup and brushed out his black curls. It had been risky adding *The Secret Child* solo at the end of the program. He wondered if anyone out there would know, would appreciate the subtle gift. Did the children know the repertoire well enough to pick that up? During their long strange talk the night before, Rutheen said they watched clips of the Merculian National Dance Company constantly, trying to emulate what they saw. It made Triani sad to think about it. Even he, a street kid peddling his ass in the Pleasure Gardens in his youth, had had good dance teachers. At their age... He couldn't bear to think about it.

He went back to his room and dressed carefully for the strange meeting. There was always the chance that they would decide not to come. He tried to imagine how he would feel in their circumstances. Did they know they were dying? Did they realize that everything they had inherited from him was killing them? Everything that was frustrating them, giving them longings they could never satisfy, came from him? His cursed genes, a double dose from the same gene pool. All because of his parent who had thought of nothing beyond his own selfish and illegal pleasure.

He punched his image in the mirror. It shattered, cutting his hand.

∞

Ten minutes later, Triani walked slowly up the hall and stood uncertainly outside the rehearsal room door. He usually timed things so that he could make a grand entrance once everyone else had arrived. But not today. At the exact time Rutheen had suggested, he clapped in the Merculian custom, then opened the door.

Rutheen sat alone in the middle of the room on one of the awful orange chairs. They must a warehouse somewhere full of the ugly things, he thought as he crossed the floor, took her hand and kissed her palm, as if they had never met before. He needed the formality to hang on to. Were the children watching him and their mother from the other side of the mirrored wall?

Rutheen seemed perfectly relaxed. "You're right on time," she said.

"I wouldn't want to be late for this," he replied, sitting down on one of the other chairs and crossing his legs at the ankle in a calculated effort to at least appear calm. "Are they coming?"

"I honestly don't know."

Triani took a deep breath. "I'll wait as long as I can, sweetie, but I can't miss my ride home."

"Oh, we wouldn't want you to do that!" exclaimed a light Merculian voice behind him.

Triani stood up. Kellan towered above him, broad, squat, with powerful shoulders and Triani's snapping round black eyes. By contrast, his hands were small, delicate, the fingers long and graceful. The other two were right behind him. Both of them had his round dark eyes, his curly black hair. The boy wore an oxygen clip over his nose. The girl looked the most Merculian because she was light-boned, but even she was taller than her father, and Triani prided himself on his height.

"Thank you for *The Secret Child* solo," she said shyly.

Triani smiled, relieved, but when he touched her hand, she pulled away.

"Mom said you offered to take us to Merculian," Kellan said, standing arms akimbo, legs wide apart, staring at Triani belligerently.

"It was just a thought," Triani said uneasily.

Kellan laughed. "You think we'd fit in there? Are you stupid as well as promiscuous?"

Triani stepped back as if hit. He hadn't expected a direct verbal attack. "Our healers might be able to help you."

"Sure, *sweetie*. You're just full of thoughtfulness and paternal love, aren't you?"

"Look, smartass! I'm sorry you're sick, but what can I do about it?"

"Just get the hell off our world."

Kellan turned away. Rutheen looked at Triani and shrugged.

"Well, do you two feel the same way about me?" Triani asked, looking from the girl to the boy. Smaller and lighter than their sibling, they were like mirror reflections of each other. It was eerie. Multiple births on Merculian were extremely rare.

"Don't pay any attention to him," the boy said. "We used to dream about you coming here. We used to plan how we would dance for you and you would help us."

"Why the hell didn't you tell me, then?" asked Triani. "I could do that. I could teach you..." His voice trailed off. How long did they have, anyway? He couldn't remember if Rutheen had said.

"It doesn't matter now," the girl said. She sat down and took a drink out of the bottle she carried at her waist. Was that medicinal, he wondered?

"You hurt your hand?" she asked.

"It's nothing." Triani glanced at the orange blood still oozing around the medi-spray bandage.

"Sarelle's always cutting herself," the boy said, standing beside his sister.

Sarelle laughed and rubbed a gash on the inside of one arm. The cut looked fresh, the blood not the dull red of humans, but bright orange. Like his.

Triani looked at Rutheen. "Have they ever needed transfusions?"

She nodded. "We've used a synthetic blend several times, but it's dangerous. Sometimes it does more harm than good."

"I'm mostly the problem," Sarelle said.

"It's a common Merculian difficulty," Triani said. "At least, I can do something about that. How much do you need?"

"You're willing to give us your blood?"

"Not all of it, sweetie."

"Oh, wonderful!" Kellan exploded. "So now you're trying to buy us with your blood? I have to admit that's original, *Chai* Triani." The scornful way he spat out the respectful Merculian form of address made Triani wince.

"Get out of here, Kellan," the boy said, turning on his sibling. "You're not the one who needs the stuff, Sarelle is. Just get out and stay out!"

"Paolo, enough. Kellan, unless you can keep a civil tongue in your head, leave." Rutheen's low voice had the effect of a cold shower on the group. Kellan looked at her incredulously, then turned around and strode out, slamming the door after him.

"He hates me, doesn't me?" Triani said bitterly.

"He hates his life," Rutheen answered.

"He's the really talented one," Paolo said. "He teaches all of us, the steps, the movements, the body language, as much as he can figure out. He even designs the scenery."

"That hothead?" Triani was impressed.

"He has endless patience where Merculian dance is concerned," said Rutheen. "Except in looks, he's the one most like you, I suspect."

"How does he learn? Who teaches him?"

"He teaches himself," Rutheen said, a note of pride in her voice. "We get all the broadcasts and clips we can, and he studies them second by second, making notations of every move. Then he teaches the children who are interested."

"Show me," said Triani, leaning forward. "Show me something you've worked on. A duet. Solo. Anything."

"*Us* dance for *you*?" Sarelle looked shocked. Her face had gone pale.

"Isn't this what you wanted?" Triani said.

"Come on, Sarelle," Paolo said. "It's a chance to see what we're doing wrong."

Triani got to his feet and went over to the music box on one wall. He flipped it on. At once, the *Prindi Nan* duet he and Eulio had danced an hour ago spilled out into the room.

"They haven't had any proper training," Rutheen said nervously, standing up.

"I know that. Sit down, Rutheen. Let them dance."

She sat down reluctantly, obviously worried about his reaction to their awkward efforts.

"We'll do our short version," Sarelle said. She was flushed now that she'd made up her mind. Paolo started the music over again and they took up their positions in the middle of the room. Paolo's lips moved as he counted down the intro.

Triani settled back in his chair, determined to suspend his usual hypercritical comments. He was a perfectionist, demanding impossibly high standards from everyone, including himself. Many members of the chorus had been reduced to tears by his stinging criticism, but this was different. Although he winced and bit his lip hard several times, he kept silent. Less than a minute into the program, however, he was leaning forward again.

"I wish I'd known about you all sooner," he murmured.

The couple danced on. After a nervous, stuttering start, they were now lost in their own world, a world they had obviously lived in for a long time. The steps were wrong more often than not, the technique needed a lot of work, but the fact that they could do it at all was astonishing. Their natural grace and instinctive feel for the music was something that could not be learned.

And then it happened. Triani saw it coming and leapt out of his chair across the room in a flash, just before Sarelle screamed. She began to fall headfirst to the ground. Instinctively, Triani reached for her waist, but the angle was wrong and he barely succeeded in sliding his own body between Sarelle and the floor. She fell on him with a thud.

"Holy shit!" Triani exclaimed, once he got his breath back. "How much do you weigh?"

"Oh God! I'm so sorry!" Sarelle quickly got to her feet. "Are you all right?"

"I'll live." Triani got up more slowly, rubbing his shoulder. "Falling is part of the job description for a dancer. Not that I've done it for a long time."

Paolo looked close to tears. Must be the Merculian in

him, Triani thought, smiling. "Look kid, it was a minor mistake. I knew she'd fall when I saw where your hands were on his waist."

"Her waist," Paolo muttered.

"Whatever. Your hands were too low and too close together. Let's walk through it."

Rutheen had turned off the music and stood watching as Triani demonstrated the right way to do the lift. "It's bio-mechanics," he said. "Work with the body every time. See?"

Paolo nodded.

"Apart from that, sweetie, it wasn't bad," he said. "I can't believe you kids haven't studied under a dance teacher."

"Just Kellan," Sarelle said, still out of breath.

Triani turned around, strode to the wall behind him and put both hands on the mirror. He could feel Kellan there on the other side, the waves of desolation coming strong to his touch. He gazed at his own reflection. "It was a brilliant adaptation," he breathed. After a moment he turned back to the small group in the room. Kellan wouldn't come back again. He would see the accident as evidence of his failure.

"Keep doing what you're doing," Triani said, taking a quick look at his chronometer. "I have to go." He glanced at the mirror one last time. How do you say goodbye to the children you never knew existed? He turned suddenly, almost blinded with tears, and headed to his room.

Eulio had already gone. Triani grabbed his long glittering coat and his shoulder bag and strode out of the room, following the corridor to the heavy doors. He pushed his way outside to the smoggy foul air of the square.

Rutheen was waiting for him there. "Thank you," she said.

"How long?"

"A few months, six at best."

"Shit."

"You weren't ever supposed to know," she said.

"Well, that didn't work out too well, did it, sweetie?"

Rutheen pulled her scarf up over her mouth.

Triani coughed and ran to catch up with Eulio, standing on the gangplank, waiting.

"Where have you been?" he asked. "Surely even you don't find these people attractive enough for sex."

"Shut up!"

Triani turned and scanned the silent crowd, looking for one face. When he saw it, he dropped his bag and rushed back down the gangplank. "Kellan!" he called. The foul air caught at the back of his throat, almost strangling him.

The fury had gone from the round black eyes, replaced by endless longing. Triani threw his arms about the hulking figure, pressing him close in a fierce embrace that was painful in its intimacy. Slowly, the youth returned the embrace, his arms like steel cables around the slim Merculian.

Finally, Triani broke away and struggled out of his glittering coat. "Take it," he said. "It's from home." He thrust the outrageously expensive garment into the boy's arms and pushed his way back to where the astonished Eulio stood watching by the open door of the shuttle.

"Well, well," Eulio said, handing Triani back his bag. "So that was your conquest. That coat of yours will never fit him, you know."

Triani glared at him. "His name is Kellan Triani Wilson."

Eulio's mouth fell open in a perfect O. If Triani was using the Merculian naming system, this could only mean one thing. "You danced *The Secret Child* for him, didn't you?"

Triani turned abruptly and stalked into the shuttle.

THE DANGER DANCE

Book One

of

THE MERCULIANS

Chapter One

Chapter One

Beny raised his head and listened, his hands poised motionless over the silver keyboards of his instrument. It wasn't a sound that had disturbed him, exactly. It was more like a whisper in the air, a feeling, as if a cool breath had passed underneath his skin. All traces of the music he had been working on vanished, pushed out of his mind by this alien something, this subtle change in the atmosphere.

The slight Merculian got to his feet and looked around the familiar room, confused. But everything was the same. The glowing blossoms of the flowering root plants made phosphorescent patterns against the glass of the underground window; the blue of the morning sky flooded in through the transparent bubble of the roof; the instruments and recording equipment were arranged around the walls of the bright workroom as always.

Uneasy now, Beny ran one small hand through his thick reddish-gold curls and decided to check with Eulio. Had he, too, felt that strange disturbance? Eulio was more finely attuned to atmosphere than most Merculians. Beny opened the door and hurried along the quiet passage. He knew Eulio would be rehearsing at this hour, stretching and toning those beautiful muscles, making them perform the impossible feats of the dance that looked so effortless on stage. He passed the courtyard with its floating garden, the brilliant changing colors swaying in the bright water, and came to the door of the rehearsal area. He could hear the music, but through the glass wall, he saw that Eulio was just standing there, wiping the sweat off the back of his neck with a towel, a puzzled expression on his face.

"You felt it, too," said Beny, opening the door. He went over to Eulio, took the towel from him and wiped his back and chest tenderly. The love jewel resting in the hollow of Eulio's throat pulsed a deep violet.

"What is it?" Eulio's blue eyes stared around the bare room as if trying to pinpoint the cause of the disturbance. He clapped his hands and the music stopped. "I was working on that bit in *Cascades* with the triple jump and I suddenly had this weird feeling, almost as if the air pressure had changed or something. I can't explain it."

"I know. I felt it, too." They looked at each other. As they touched, each could sense clearly the feelings and emotions of the other. "You'd better get dressed, love."

"But I've only been working for an hour." Eulio blinked, feeling his lover's unexpressed fear. "Wait for me," he said and slipped into the change room next door. Beny heard the hiss of the shower, the snap of the clothing recycler accepting the sweaty rehearsal tights.

Why am I afraid in my own house? Beny thought, beginning to pace. This had never happened to him before. He was proud of his house. Here, he had collected the things that were most dear to him: exquisite, hand-crafted examples of the instruments he loved, several original paintings illustrating the Merculian Dragon Legends, the many prizes he had brought back from music festivals, the Certificates of Excellence in Language Studies, his hard-won diploma from the I.P.A. Academy. In the past few blissful months, the house was growing to reflect the life of Eulio as well. Witness to this was the room Beny was pacing around in now, which had been part of the garden before Eulio had accepted his love jewel and agreed to share his life for a time. It was because of this that his music was better than ever. He knew that the dances he wrote for Eulio would make him Merculian's leading musician. But now… Where had this insidious, ominous tingle of dread come from?

"I'm ready." Eulio stood in the doorway. He wore a long white robe that was open to the waist, showing off his smooth, muscled chest. Beny resisted the urge to touch him, knowing that would only reinforce their unease.

"Let's check the house," he said. "We'll ask the Keeper if he's noticed anything."

As they walked through the deceptively peaceful rooms, sunk into the ground to retain their coolness yet open to the almost perpetual daylight of their planet, they kept close together. Neither spoke.

The Keeper, when they found him, appeared annoyed to see them. He was cleaning the food synthesizer and did not want to be disturbed at this difficult task.

"I have no idea what you mean, *Chai* Benvolini," he said coolly, withdrawing his head from the complicated intestines of the synthesizer. "I can assure you that the androids are all in working order and the air-circulating system was checked just last week. Could it be something to do with the gardeners?"

Beny wanted to point out that the gardeners were supposed to be part of the Keeper's job as well, but he let it go. "Perhaps we're just oversensitive," he said with a smile. The Keeper sniffed and disappeared back into the synthesizer.

"Why don't we fire him?" suggested Eulio when they were out of earshot.

"I can't. He came with the house."

"He doesn't like me," Eulio said, amazed. He wasn't used to people not liking him. He was one of Merculian's leading dancers, a star with the National Dance Company. He was used to adulation.

They made their way to the front of the house where the water from the ornamental pool outside pressed against the wall of glass, dappling the rooms inside with a constantly shifting pattern of light. Suddenly, they both stopped. Beny felt something prickle along the back of his neck. There, in the main reception area was…a presence. Beny glanced at Eulio. Standing together in the doorway, they bowed low before the Praetan of Merculian.

The High Priest was alone, yet he seemed to fill every space in the room. He sat with his back to the round window, his deep purple robe spread about him in stiff folds. The sunlight filtering through the water behind the glass formed a glancing halo around his head. He was a timeless figure, his age a matter of conjecture only. His skin, thin like tissue paper over a layer of dough, gave the impression that if touched, a permanent indentation would result. The round eyes were colorless.

"Greetings, Orosin At'hali Benvolini." The voice grated, as if it were seldom used, making Beny's full official name sound ominous.

"Greetings, Praetan." Beny swallowed, his eyes fixed on the thick greenish band that hung loosely around the High Priest's neck. Now he understood that it was a security probe that they had felt.

"Come closer. My sight is not what it used to be."

They crossed the room together and stood before him. Beny could feel beads of sweat dampening the hair at his temples. The auricular membranes protected by his thick curls started to hurt as they often did when he was under pressure. What have I done? he thought. What have I left undone?

"May light shine upon you always," intoned the Praetan, sketching a circle above their bowed heads. He reached out and touched the jewel around Eulio's neck. It turned a sickly shade of yellow. "I see that what I have to say will concern both of you now." He paused, and Beny felt the tension twist in his stomach. He opened his mouth to speak, but the Praetan silenced him with a gesture.

"I understand that you went to the Academy of the Inter Planetary Alliance, Orosin."

"I…ah, yes. It was years ago. I did not distinguish myself."

"As a people, our talents lie elsewhere, which is why it is unusual for a Merculian to go to the Academy at all, much less make it through. Your ambition speaks well for you."

"I only did it to please my parents, Praetan. They have great faith in the role of Merculian in the Alliance."

"And you do not?"

"Oh yes, of course, I do! But I am a musician."

"You got to know many people there from all cultures and races and species, I understand."

"My classmates, yes. I had several roommates, too: a Terran female, an Elutian, a Serpian male."

"And you got along well with all of them."

"I tried, but the Elutian was difficult. They have to have moisture on their skin all the time, you know, and the climate there was very dry. He was cranky because he was uncomfortable a lot of the time, and I kept having nightmares that I might wake up and find him dehydrated and wrinkled up past recognition. I was relieved when he left. The Serpian, Thar-von Del, became a friend, though. We went through a lot together."

"We have followed your career with great interest. You have represented Merculian well in both the musical field and in the Academy. Now Merculian needs your help."

Beny shuddered. The band around the High Priest's neck began to undulate and glow. Beny stared in horror, unable to tear his eyes away.

"Come closer. We will not be disturbed." He paused as the two took a small step forward. "You are going on tour soon with the dance company, are you not, Eulio?"

"Yes, Praetan. In two days. We'll be visiting some Terran colonies and performing on board the I.P.A. starship *Wellington* in between stopovers."

"I see. The entire company is going?"

"The senior company only, and one apprentice, I think."

"You, Orosin, you will be going as well?"

"I would love to, Praetan, but I…I have to finish the prelude music for the Water Festival."

It was as if the Praetan had not heard him. "I have a mission for you. We have reason to believe that there is a spy on board the *Wellington*, passing top secret information about fleet movements and new weaponry to our enemies in the Troia. Bringing in an outside investigator would alert this person instantly, but who would suspect a young Merculian reservist officer and his pretty dancer lover?"

Beny jerked his head back, feeling as if he had been struck. He stared at this almost mythic being. The Praetan had been part of the fabric of his young life: a mystical, shadowy presence in the background on many ceremonial occasions. The great power of his position sprang from a potent combination of the seen and the unseen that captured the imagination and caught at the dark places in the soul. Now Beny remembered the whispers, vague rumors about the Praetan's clandestine machinations that reached far beyond their own planet, and he was determined that he and Eulio would not become part of this far-flung web of intrigue.

"Praetan, I am sorry, but we can't do this! Besides, we wouldn't be any good at all! You implied as much yourself!"

There was no answer. The circular band had separated itself into a line now, and was oozing across the High Priest's neck toward his shoulder.

Beny felt the room spin. He reached out and took Eulio's hand. It was cold. He wanted to shout at the Praetan, this creature whom he had never actually seen up close before. He wanted to scream *No! By whose authority do you give me these orders?*

He moistened his lips. "Praetan," he began carefully, "all my life I have been taught to honor and respect you. But this mission with Eulio…forgive me, but I do not understand how you can—"

"You question my authority?"

"Oh no! Certainly not! It's just…well…I mean…."

He could feel the High Priest looking at him as the silence pulsed around them. The snakelike creature undulated along the Praetan's arm and suspended itself from his wrist, swaying hypnotically back and forth.

Beny felt a wave of nausea.

"I am just a musician," he went on desperately. He felt the sweat between his shoulder blades. "That's all. I have not joined the Service, nor do I ever intend to."

"And you have not performed your compulsory tour of duty to the Alliance."

Beny's heart sank and his fingers tingled unpleasantly. It was true. Every graduate of the Academy was expected to spend a term serving on board a starship of the I.P.A. fleet. Beny's family had enough diplomatic connections to have had this unpleasant duty postponed indefinitely. It was his reward for actually making it through the highly technical course of studies.

Beny cleared his throat. "My tour of duty has been waived."

"Everyone must serve. It is the law."

"But…I have other commitments now."

Silence.

Beny's eyes darted around the room, as if in search of inspiration. He glanced at Eulio, standing motionless beside him.

"All right," he said, his voice hoarse. "You want me to be a spy? I'll do it, on one condition."

"Do you try to bargain with me?"

"Oh no! But…I mean it's not necessary to involve Eulio. He has nothing to do with the Inter Planetary Alliance."

"I can speak for myself, Orosin," said Eulio suddenly, dropping his hand. "If you are involved in this thing, then so am I."

The Praetan's lip curled up slightly at one side. He glanced at Eulio, then back to Beny. "Terrans have great curiosity about hermaphrodites like us. Your looks should be an advantage in getting information. You will do what is necessary, of course."

"But—"

"You have heard, no doubt, of The Watchers?" The words seemed to come out of the air, rather than from his mouth.

Beny nodded hopelessly. So that was it. This secret network was said to be far-reaching indeed, the identity of their leaders shrouded in mystery. It was impossible to get any definite information about them. If the Praetan was one of them, there was no recourse to any higher authority.

"But what are we supposed to do exactly?" faltered Eulio, as the silence threatened to extend itself indefinitely.

"Someone is sending information to the Troia and it is coming from the *Wellington*, the ship the dance company is scheduled to travel on. This has been going on for about three months now. We want to know what this information is and who is sending it."

"But, Praetan, the ship leaves in two days. How can Orosin—"

"Everything is arranged. And remember, this is top secret. You are to confide in no one."

"What about the Captain?" asked Beny. "Can we talk to him?"

"No one. The captain will be informed at the proper time. Let him contact you. And remember, no one is above suspicion. Everyone has a price."

Beny drew an outraged breath.

"Don't be naive, Benvolini." The dangling snake thing swung toward him, and Beny drew back. "Everybody has a weakness: a mate, a lover, a child, a career, something that makes them vulnerable. There is always a weak link in any chain. Think of yourself for a moment. Would you not do anything—anything at all—for this pretty little one?" His voice trailed off into silence. One dry, bony finger was pointing at Eulio.

Beny clasped his hands together and said nothing. He could feel Eulio beside him physically recoil from the condescension in that cool thread of a voice.

"You will send your reports Merculian code 16 to the Council," the voice continued. "It will be relayed to I.P.A. Headquarters from this end."

"What if something awful happens?" asked Eulio at last.

"Then, and only then, play this disc." A small yellow rectangle slid to the floor in front of them. Eulio picked it up. "And remember, I was never here. You will never even mention my name."

Beny and Eulio bowed low. For a moment, it was as if a cool, shuddering breeze passed by beside them. When they looked up again, the room was empty.

About the Author

Caro Soles has written in many genres, as is obvious from these stories. Her novels include mystery, science fiction, adventure and espionage, and literary. She received a Derrick Murdoch Award from the Crime Writers of Canada and has been shortlisted for a Lambda Literary Award, an Aurora Award, and a Stoker Award. Caro lives in Toronto and loves dachshunds, books, opera and ballet, not necessarily in that order. Her new book, *Marlo's Dance*, is another in her SF series featuring the pleasure-loving hermaphrodites of Merculian and will be out in 2020.

Also by Caro Soles:
The Tangled Boy
A Mutual Understanding
Drag Queen in the Court of Death
A Friend of Mr. Nijinsky
People Like Us
The Danger Dance
The Abulon Dance
The Memory Dance
Marlo's Dance (out from Crossroad Press, 2020)
Dancing With Chairs in the Music House (coming in fall 2020 from Inanna Publications)

(AUTHOR'S NOTE: Alas, in spite of many of these titles, I do not dance, but I love watching others perform!)

ALSO FROM BASKERVILLE BOOKS

The Wild Hunt, a vampire novella by Nancy Kilpatrick

And coming soon:

Vampyre Theatre by Nancy Kilpatrick